THE CIVIL WAR OF Amos Abernathy

THE CIVIL WAR OF
Amos Abernathy

MICHAEL LEALI

HARPER
An Imprint of HarperCollinsPublishers

ISBN 978-0-06-311986-4

Typography by Corina Lupp
22 23 24 25 26   SB   10 9 8 7 6 5 4 3 2 1

First Edition

For Mom and Dad

1

Sunday, August 15, 2021

Dear Albert,

Writing letters to dead people isn't something I usually do, but this feels weirdly... right? I don't know how to explain it exactly. It's like even as I wrote the words "Dear Albert," I felt like maybe, just maybe, you could hear me. Which I know is ridiculous, but I sort of need you to hear me.

Ever since I was a little kid, like eight years old, I've volunteered at the Chickaree County Living History Park as a nineteenth-century historical reenactor. People like to walk through the grounds and dream about that "simpler time," but they have NO IDEA. There's nothing simple about growing and harvesting (and *killing*) your own food or having to make anything you want from scratch, and don't even get me started on the lack of indoor plumbing. Not to mention slavery and racism and white people stealing land from Native Americans. I guess what I'm saying is, I get that life back then wasn't easy.

Don't get me wrong. I love reenacting—almost everything about it. When I put on my pioneer costume, it's like time traveling. For a little while there's no cell phones or social media and it's just me and a butter churn. The leaves are brighter, the sun's warmer, the birds are louder.

I've always felt like I've belonged at the Living History Park. You see, Mom's been the lead interpreter (which is sort of like the manager) since I was born, so it's always been a homestead away from home. She organizes all the volunteers and oversees restorations, and I've been by her side for almost all of it. The nineteenth century is in my blood.

So, maybe it's only natural that I have a nineteenth-century pen pal! If I'm being honest, though, I didn't just *decide* to begin writing you letters. All of this started because of Ben Oglevie. Maybe I should tell you about him first.

I met Ben in March at this year's junior volunteer orientation, sitting in an icebreaker circle on the floor of New Hope Church (built in 1874). Most of us junior volunteers have been at it for years, but every now and then someone new shows up. Ben Oglevie was one of only two fresh recruits, so of course Mom put them both in *my* group, because I'm essentially the one-boy welcoming committee for new volunteers. (Yay for perks of being the boss's kid.) ANYWAY, Ben's sitting across from me, all elbows and knees, chin nearly tucked under his arm like a chicken settling in for the night. *Cool, cool, cool,* I think. *Another kid who doesn't want to be here.* (The other new kid, this pale freckled girl named Samantha, quit by the end of May.)

After we said our names and a pizza topping to match (I was "Anchovy Amos"), we went around and shared why we wanted to be historical reenactors.

Samantha: My mom is making me.

(See what I mean, Albert?)

Ben: I like history. Um, a lot.

Okay. Not a my-parents-made-me-do-it kid. Maybe he's just shy? I could work with that.

Yada yada yada—the get-to-know-you questions went on, until we got to my favorite one: "What historical figure do you think you know more about than anyone else in the circle?"

Samantha: Uh, I don't know. No one?

(UGH.)

Ben: Abraham Lincoln.

I mentally cracked my knuckles. Um, Abe, one of the most famous people from Illinois, is *my* guy. So, I said, "Let's see what you got. When was he born?"

"February 12, 1809. In Kentucky. Near Hodgenville."

I didn't ask for city and state—a bit of a show-off, but okay. "How many siblings did he have?"

"Two. Sarah and Tommy."

The other kids' eyes bounced between us as I fired off another question. The longer we went back and forth, the more excited I got. Somehow, I ended up crouched like a frog. Ben, though—he started to unfold, limbs relaxing, stretching out.

Since it looked like he was getting too comfortable, I lobbed a real corkscrew. "Abe's in the hall of fame for what athletic event?"

That was the first time I saw him smile. Kind of crooked. Goofy. But he held my stare. "Wrestling."

I fell back on my behind and smiled. "Bingo."

After *that* display, he pretty much had no choice but to be my friend.

I'd pegged Ben as shy, but it turned out he's just one of those quiet, observant types that's thinking a million miles a minute, and all of his thoughts are deep, existential thoughts, not just, "I think I want a turkey sandwich instead of ham." It might be because he's homeschooled, but I don't want to stereotype.

Lucky for me, Ben and I were able to work most of the same shifts (knowing the person in charge *does* occasionally have its benefits). I introduced him to my best friend, Chloe Thompson, and it was instantly like the three of us had always been together. Ben and I went to most of Chloe's softball games in April. The three of us became regulars at the ice cream shop downtown—he and Chloe really bonded over their shared passion for coconut ice cream (ewww). We even have a pact to shave our heads if any of us decides to ditch our friend group.

Just kidding. BUT WE SO WOULD.

So, okay, here's the other thing about Ben . . .

Wow.

This shouldn't be THAT hard to say. But, I mean, I guess I've never said it about anyone I actually know, so . . .

Okay, Amos. You got this.

Here it is: Ben's cute.

Like, *really* cute. He's a little taller than me, and white with blond hair. He has eyes like old pennies, and I mean that in a good way. They're a million shades of brown—copper and chocolate and mud—and they're always watching. Sometimes, when he's working on something, I just like to watch him paying attention to whatever he's doing. He's got a dimple on his right cheek. A square chin. And there's something about the way his neck meets his body, like he just comes together in this seamless way that's smooth and sharp all at the same time. But it's his collarbone that really does it for me.

There. I said it.

AAAAHHHHH!

Albert, I've thought before that boys, in general, are cute, but I've never said a *specific* boy is cute. Honestly, I didn't even think Ben was *that* good-looking at first. The weirdest thing in the world changed my mind. It was mid-June—oh my god, this is going to sound so dumb, Albert—and Chloe, Ben, and I were at the LHP walking from the Wakefield House, this grayish building that used to be a doctor's office, to the homestead. Ben had a stick, and he was dragging it along the wrought iron fence, which Chloe legit thinks is beautiful—she's obsessed with anything that comes out of a blacksmith shop—and then suddenly he had two sticks and the *tick*, *tick*, *tick* turned into *tick*, *ticka-tok*, *ticka-tok* as he drummed along the posts.

I laughed. "What are you doing?"

"What's it look like?" The sticks jumped from the fence to my shoulders. He grinned and said, "Making music."

I shook him off and called him weird, still laughing. But that was the moment. It was like waking up. My heart wouldn't slow down. I got goose bumps. It was weird.

I felt WEIRD.

So, now it's been months of this me-watching-him-watch-things . . . *thing*, and I don't know what to do. I feel like I should have good gaydar, but maybe I'm not gay enough? I don't know. I've been out since fourth grade, but living in the semirural Midwest really puts my abilities to the test. I mean, I've got the internet and I've watched all of *Glee* twice, so I know *some* things about being gay, but it really wasn't until middle school that I had a sort of community.

Our Gender and Sexuality Alliance is awesome, and my friends from the GSA are cool, but none of them are super into history like I am. The point is that I've only had so much practice around people like me, so I'm not always sure how to read other people or talk about gay things.

Then, a couple of weeks ago, this happened.

It was Saturday, and Ben and I were sitting on the porch of the Wakefield House. We were playing jacks and laughing about something, and then we both reached for the ball at the same time and our fingers touched for half a second too long to be normal. I pulled my hand back right away, afraid he might freak. (Stuff like that's happened to me before.)

But his hand kind of stayed there, and then he looked up at me with his penny eyes and just stared.

My cheeks felt like toasted marshmallows. I couldn't read his expression, so I blurted, "What?"

He shook his head. "Nothing."

I shook mine right back. "No, not nothing. Why were you looking at me like that?"

"Like what? I was just, uh, looking at your face."

I thought to myself, *Okay, he's either way weirder than I realized, or . . .*

His hand pulled back, dragging a jack between his fingers. His right knee bounced. "I just mean you have a nice face," he added quickly.

"Thanks?"

Birds chirped. My heart thrummed in my ears. A trio of elderly white women walked by and waved. We waved back. They kept walking.

Then I made things even more awkward and said, "You also have a face that is nice."

ALBERT.

YOU ALSO HAVE A FACE THAT IS NICE? This was the point where I wanted to crawl under the porch and die from embarrassment, but before I could ooze away, Ben said, "You really think so?"

"I mean, yeah, you have a really nice face. Not that I'm the judge of all faces or that my opinion counts for anything, but—wait, what? Are you laughing at me?" I was saying WAY too much. Sometimes that happens when I'm nervous.

His lips twisted into a squiggle, but he couldn't keep the smile from his eyes. They were wide and shining and still watching me.

"No, I just—I don't know, I really like your face," he said.

I leaned back. The single jack wove between his fingers. He watched it roll over his knuckles, and I watched him watching it, hoping for some clue about what I should say next.

I got nothing.

Finally, I said, "Are you—are you saying what I think you're saying?"

He twisted to the side, like he was cracking his back, but I'm pretty sure he just wanted to make sure we were alone. He spun back around. "What do you mean? What are *you* saying?"

My words fell out a syllable at a time. "I think I'm saying that maybe I like your face as much as you might like my face, and that by *like* I mean *like-like*, not just like . . . you know, *like?*"

Ben's chest expanded with an inhale. He got all pale. His head nodded over and over, and his breath came out in a slow, steady stream.

"Oh." He sounded hurt. Offended.

I panicked. "I'm sorry if I'm wrong. I didn't mean to—"

He shook his head. "No, no! Amos, I—I just . . . I'm not . . ." He swallowed.

Aaaaand now my insides were screaming: RUN. FIND A HOLE. BURY YOURSELF FOR ALL ETERNITY. THE END. I pushed off the porch and said, "Never mind."

He called after me. "Amos! Where are you going? I didn't mean—"

"Bathroom!" I yelled, not looking back. "Urgent!"

Um, I hate to do this to you, Albert, but the situation has become urgent again.

Be right back!

2

Homestead Exhibit
Saturday, August 13, 2022—9:00 a.m.

Today is either going to be the best or worst day of my life. Even with all the planning this past year, all the research, the thinking, the conversations—the *drama*—there's this hollowness I can't shake. Something's off. Something's missing.

No, not some*thing*—some*one*.

I stab a fire-bitten log in the grate with an iron poker.

Freaking Ben Oglevie.

For months now, the boy who got all this started one year ago hasn't said a word to me. Complete and utter silence. It's like he never existed, like smoke vanishing in a breeze; but that's how he showed up, too—the way fireworks just kind of burst out of the darkness.

But that was then. I'm not some naive twelve-year-old anymore. I'm thirteen, a *teenager*. I know better. Soon I won't even be a junior volunteer anymore. By nineteenth-century standards, turning thirteen makes me a man. Even though it's the twenty-first century, we historical reenactors of the Chickaree County Living History Park play by nineteenth-century rules.

Well, for the most part. I hadn't thought about it until this past year (hello, White Privilege), but until lately we haven't thought much about the color of a volunteer's skin. How race plays into our portrayal of history. Slavery and racism were *definitely* a thing in nineteenth-century Illinois, but here, anyone can live as a free person did, it doesn't matter the color of your skin. It's great that we're inclusive . . . but by being inclusive, we've sort of been ignoring the awful truth about our past, and that's messed up.

Obviously, all of these are rules I've come to question. And I don't know if that would have happened if my friends—*friend*—and I hadn't poked around embers of history nearly snuffed out. Maybe if it wasn't for Freaking Ben Oglevie, we'd all be transitioning to apprentice volunteers without a care in the world.

But now there's no Ben. And my future as a historical reenactor depends on how everything goes down this afternoon on the main stage. So does Chloe's, and it's not *her* mom who's in charge. I've got extra protection that she doesn't, and she's already been through way too much this past year. I poke at a burning log. Three o'clock is six short hours away. Somehow that feels like forever and way too soon.

The fire spits. A fresh whoosh of heat slaps my cheek. I hang the iron poker on the wall of the one-room log cabin.

Today the rules change. For better or worse, and maybe a whole lot worse, Chloe and I are going to make history—*change* history, make history *right*—if it's the very last thing we ever do as historical reenactors.

Gravel crunches. My head turns. For the briefest moment, I think, *Ben*. But it's just Darren Blake coming through the back door of the log cabin.

"Gonna get that demo set up?" he says. "We've got a summer camp coming through first thing."

"Yeah, I'm on it."

Junior volunteers always have an adult volunteer supervising their exhibit, even if they will be apprentice volunteers at the end of the season. . . . Anyway, this morning, my supervisor just so happens to be my band teacher, my percussion instructor, and my mom's boyfriend. Darren's a little bit lumberjack, a little bit nerd. White, with broad shoulders and a beer belly. His hair's thinning, but not in one of those unlucky horseshoes. All in all, he's not that bad looking, but it's beyond weird to think of your teacher/your mom's boyfriend as "attractive." Gross.

I know I should be used to the idea of them being together at this point, but I'm not.

He looks at me funny. "You doing all right, Amos?"

"Yeah, I'm fine. Just hot." And mad. And worried that this might be the last time I ever work at the homestead exhibit. That I'm making life harder for Chloe.

"Tell me about it. I'd be grateful for a little cloud cover." He peeks out the back door, squinting. "I'm gonna get a fire started in the pit. Holler if you need help with the candles."

"Will do." I give him a lazy salute and he disappears out the door.

And thoughts of Ben walk right back in. Even after what he said to me, even after so much silence, I'd rather have him here than not.

I kind of hate that I feel that way.

A log breaks in the flames and a wedge of ruby wood tumbles from the grate. I kick it back in. No way am I going to be blamed for burning down the log cabin that's been painstakingly patched up since 1826 because I got distracted by thoughts of Ben Oglevie.

I run my fingers through my hair. The dark brown, wavy mess of a mop drips into my eyes. I draw my arm across my forehead, and the blue fabric comes away a shade darker with sweat.

Ew.

It's got to be close to eighty degrees already, and this freaking fire isn't helping. I roll back the sleeves of my shirt past my elbows and undo the button below my chin. Wet spots dot my chest and armpits. Normally I'd freak about pitting out, but people visit the LHP for authenticity. From the buildings to the sweat stains, everything is true to fact. Well, except for nineteenth-century racism. And body odor. Thank God Mom hasn't banned deodorant.

I try to put Ben (and three o'clock) out of my mind by setting up the candle-making demonstration. I go through the day's schedule in my head. First, I'm stationed here at the homestead exhibit; then it's off to the Wakefield House; the schoolhouse; the battle reenactment; the printshop; and then, finally, the main stage.

My heart flutters.

Focus, Amos. Candles.

Most interpreters at the homestead show folks how to make tallow candles, but I can't stand the smell, like bacon gone bad. Visitors don't stay long on days we practice that much authenticity. Seems to me people like the *idea* of experiencing the "real thing" but not the *actual* thing itself once it's in front of them. If history isn't comfortable, a lot of people don't want to look at it . . . or smell it.

That's why I go with beeswax. I toss a handful of

yellowish chunks into an iron skillet and stir slowly so they won't burn. While they melt, I take down the candle mold that looks like six long, skinny fingers pressed together. With my pocketknife, I snip a string of wick into equal lengths and set them in the molds. I cut a few extra to make dip candles, which are always more fun for visitors. Little kids especially like those.

As the last bit of solid wax disappears, someone knocks at the door. My heart kick-starts again, but it's only Chloe, standing in the rectangular frame. She is tall and Black, with warm bronze-colored skin and a smile that always makes me feel like I've come home. Her black, curly hair, usually long and down past her shoulders, is pulled back in a tight, shiny bun. Her pressed, corn-yellow dress falls all the way to her dusty black shoes. Twin lines of sweat slip down her temples. She dabs them away with the corner of her shawl, the periwinkle one she crocheted last winter after her grandma Justine passed away.

"You ready for today?" she asks, setting her basket on the wood table.

"Are you?"

"I asked first."

I pull the pan away from the fire but leave it near the flames to keep warm. I shove my haversack off the bench and sit down, elbows thudding on the table.

15

"I mean, *technically* I'm ready. As of this morning, no one's backed out, and everything's in place, so I guess—I guess we're really doing this. But . . . I'm nervous."

"Me, too," Chloe says. "I barely slept."

That doesn't make me feel better. "You don't have to go through with this afternoon. I know it's different for me to pull something like—"

"Amos, thanks, and I mean it"—she grabs my hand—"but I'm in this with you. This is what we do."

She's right. I think about last year in math when Joyce Hubert kept making fun of Chloe for being the only person to answer our teacher's questions. Every time Chloe even looked like she *might* raise her hand, Joyce would start snickering and looking at her friends like "Oh my god, such a nerd." It was getting so bad that Chloe stopped talking in class at all. So, I did two things: 1) I started raising *my* hand so she wasn't alone, and 2) I told Joyce, in front of all her friends at lunch, that I knew why she made fun of Chloe—it was easier to make fun of the smart kid than admit she didn't know how to find the area of a triangle. That shut her up.

I smile and squeeze Chloe's hand back. "I know this is what we do, but this could seriously mess up everything you've worked for."

"I know," she says, "but what we're doing this afternoon—that's part of making things right, and I want to be a part of that."

16

After a pause I say, "I appreciate that. A lot."

"What are best friends for?" She smiles.

I'm feeling a little better, but there's still a nagging thought bouncing around my brain. "I keep wondering if my mom suspects anything," I say.

"Why?" Her eyes widen. "You didn't let something slip, did you?"

"Of course not! I learned my lesson. She can't know a thing."

Chloe pats the perspiration from her forehead again. "I need some water."

I grab the pitcher from the mantel as Chloe pulls a tin cup from her basket. I pour her cup full and then dig through my haversack for my own. All junior volunteers are required to carry essentials in period-appropriate containers. Girls swing baskets and boys haul haversacks—these ugly square canvas bags with a long shoulder strap. Essentially, a nineteenth-century man purse. At all times, junior volunteers are to have: a tin cup, a small slate chalkboard, chalk pens that look like those old-timey candy cigarettes (they don't taste like them), an apple, and a book wrapped in brown paper (to maintain the nineteenth-century illusion).

I down my water in a single gulp. "How are the crowds so far? Darren says we've got a group coming here first thing."

"Lots of families coming through the entrance. Couple

of Girl Scout troops and a church group near the print-shop. Deborah's already complaining. But it's about what we usually get for opening day of CWRW, I guess."

CWRW—Civil War Remembrance Week—is a seven-day festival the LHP puts on every August to honor the men and women who fought during the American Civil War. People come from all over the country for pie contests, homemade sarsaparilla, and crafters who sell genuine nineteenth-century goods: watches, dressers, tables, chairs, petticoats. But the biggest draw is the battle reenactment the afternoon of opening day, a blood-spewing theatrical massacre a huge crowd gathers to watch. Men, and a few women, dress in Confederate gray and Union blue and duke it out with rifles, revolvers, and muskets.

I used to *live* for Civil War Remembrance Week, and maybe some part of me still does, but it's different now. Thanks to Chloe (. . . and Ben). Thanks to Albert. It's like I see colors I missed before. Understand the world on a level I hadn't when I was little, when I ate too much rock candy and listened to the drummer boys play, making me feel like I'd slipped back in time.

"I hope people came prepared," I say. "This heat's gonna be unbearable." I nudge Chloe's leg gently under the table. "Are you sure you're not regretting your decision about helping me? I don't want you to lose your apprenticeship."

"Are you kidding me? How many times do I have to tell

you I'm doing this because I want to?" She leans across the table, eyes shifting to the doorway. "Did you ever decide about texting Ben?"

I shrink away. "Ugh, yeah. I tried again last night, but I got nothing." I shake my head. "I'm pathetic. Ghosted by a kid who didn't even know what ghosting was until I told him. How messed up is that?" My voice lowers. "I don't know why I keep trying."

"You're not pathetic. You *care*. And Ben could still come around, you know?"

"How long am I supposed to wait for that?"

She shrugs, fidgeting with the fringe of her shawl. "Who knows! But I'm a glass-half-full kind of girl. I mean, after all the work we've done . . . if he knew, you'd think he'd at least show up for today."

I blink away the memory of the last time I saw Ben. That look on his face, the jagged edge in his voice. "Yeah, I don't know about that."

Still, there's always this annoying lingering hope. That maybe today will be different. Maybe Ben *will* answer my texts, and things will go back to the way they were before I messed everything up.

"Fine." Chloe sniffs. "You do you. I'm just saying, the Amos I know doesn't give up without a fight."

"I've *been* fighting, Chloe." I shove myself up from the table, slinging my empty tin cup back into my haversack.

I pull out my battered brown leather journal. Chloe leans her chin over the table, lips pressed together judgmentally. I choose not to notice her stare as I flip through the pages.

Chloe says. "Did Albert finally write you back?"

Cue the eyeroll. "Just making sure I've got everything memorized for today. I don't want to mess this up, too."

She stands with a sigh and squeezes my arm. "Amos, you're not the one who messed things up."

I wish that was true.

3

Sunday, August 15, 2021

Sorry, Albert! I'm back.

Where were we? Oh yeah—a cute boy and a fake break for the bathroom. UGH.

The LHP isn't *that* big, so there was no way I could avoid Ben the rest of the day, but I did manage not to get too close to him until the end of our shift.

Even though Mom's my ride and I don't leave until she does, I always hang with Chloe and the other volunteers while they wait to get picked up. Of course, that included Ben. When I walked up to the group, he smiled and said, "You make it to the bathroom all right?" like nothing ever happened.

"Ha ha, yeah, I'm good."

I couldn't decide if I was more relieved or disappointed that he was acting normal while I felt like I'd downed a bucket of awkward sauce. I kept waiting for Ben to shoot me a look or something, but NOPE. His dad showed up in their

21

minivan right before Chloe's mom got there. I was kind of hoping that it would end up just being me and Ben for a minute. But then it was just me and Chloe, and I still didn't know what Ben's "I really like your face" comment meant.

Albert, I know this is getting a little long, but I promise I'm getting to why the heck I'm writing a letter to a dead person really, really soon. So, here we go—fast-forward to this past Sunday, about a week after the Nice Face Fiasco.

At the monthly all-staff LHP meeting, Mom made a huge announcement. Chloe, Ben, and I were sitting in a pew in the back of New Hope Church with the other junior volunteers. Of course, Meredith Simmons was there with her friend Mindy Liu. Meredith is white and majorly spoiled. Mindy is Chinese American and always gives out the best valentines. She has warm, tan-colored skin and inky black hair. They sat in the back, whispering to each other the whole time. Other than the fact that she willingly chooses to spend her free time with Meredith, I have nothing against Mindy. But Meredith Simmons is the actual WORST. Not only has she tried to sabotage me since fourth grade, but she's also the queen of one-upping and the heiress to some multimillion-dollar business her great-grandfather started, which she never lets you forget. Her parents used their inheritance to start a chain of high-end shoe stores. (You have all that money, and you invest in *shoes*?!)

Folks in Chickaree County treat the Simmonses like

royalty, and it makes me want to barf slugs. They're just people. Maybe they have a lot of money, and maybe they have roots in Apple Grove from a million years ago, but that doesn't mean they get to rule the world.

Clearly, I have a lot of feelings about Meredith—which usually get me into trouble.

I was *going* to tell you what Mom said.

She stood at the podium with her iPad and scrolled through her notes as she spoke. The park was closed for the day, but Mom was still wearing her costume. Sometimes I think she's more comfortable in her long nineteenth-century dresses than modern clothes.

"The last item on our agenda has to do with the 'Heroes of the Nineteenth Century' exhibit in the main gallery. After five years, the board has decided it's time to refresh the exhibit and swap it out for something new. That's where you all come in."

Albert, did you ever get chills when you knew something was meant to be? A sort of electric tingling in your hands and feet? That's how I felt when Mom talked. And I wasn't the only one. Whispers crept up and down the pews almost immediately. (Yes, we're all a bunch of giant nerds—I love it.)

Mom waved a hand to hush us. Behind her, though, Mr. Simmons, Meredith's dad and the park's largest financial contributor, whispered something that made two board members burst out laughing. Mom cut him a firm but courteous "be quiet" look and went on: "The board wants to make this a community project. So, until Sunday, November seventh, we'll be accepting proposals for what the new exhibit should be. As dedicated volunteers of the Living History Park and avid historians in your own right, I wanted you all to be the first to know. Some of the best ideas could come from within our own ranks." Mom looked at me when she said that, like it was meant for me. "Specific details for proposal requirements can be found on the LHP website, but feel free to ask me any questions you might have."

Meredith Simmons's pink hand blinked into the air faster than a lightning strike, but she didn't wait for Mom to call on her. "Can *anyone* put a proposal together, Ms. Abernathy?"

Behind Mom, Mr. Simmons beamed. "Yes, Meredith," Mom said, "proposals from all Chickaree County community members are welcome, yourself included."

Meredith's smile took up her whole face. She spun her neck around so everyone in the church could see her joy, as if Mom had just declared that her proposal had already won.

As soon as the meeting was over, I pulled Chloe and Ben aside.

Things with Ben had been weird but okay. Like, whenever possible we still worked at the same exhibits, and he

24

always waited for me to say goodbye before he left the park. But we hadn't talked about what happened on the porch of the Wakefield House. It was driving me bananas.

I said, "We need to come up with an idea for the new exhibit. No way am I letting Meredith Simmons win. You two in?"

"Obviously!" Chloe said. "We should totally do something about the history of softball, like, going all the way from cricket to baseball. We could have a whole wall of different bats and balls, and maybe they'd even let us set up a batting cage by the fort so it's like an *interactive* exhibit! Wouldn't that be awesome?"

"Ummmmm, maybe?" I said, even though I was so not into that idea.

Chloe has this thing for loud activities. Cricket, this weird British version of baseball that was big in America during the 1800s, is her favorite sport, right after softball. Like, if there were major leagues for cricket in the United States, Chloe would be at every game.

"Oookay," she said. "How about blacksmithing, then?"

Then there's blacksmithing. Chloe's grandpa was an ironworker, a welder I think, and her dad is a construction foreman. Mr. Thompson's always talking about how important the trades are. Chloe's older sister, Cadence, is one of those doesn't-need-to-study-is-talented-at-everything people, so Chloe's always looking for a way to get her dad's attention. He thought it was cool that we have a real black-smith shop at the LHP, so now Chloe is determined to learn EVERYTHING she can about it.

Before I could answer, Ben asked, "How about skittles?"

Speaking of weird obsessions: ever since he started volunteering, Ben can't get enough of the game (not the candy). He's even building his own board as one of his homeschool projects.

"This has to be about something more important than skittles, Ben."

He crossed his arms. "There is nothing more important than skittles, Amos."

I tried my best to avoid staring at the adorable, soft curve of his pout. I pulled Chloe and Ben into a huddle, which didn't help because I got a strong whiff of him (like, in a good way), so I stopped and backed away like someone farted, but that just made it super awkward. All I could think about was the way Ben smelled. Like his deodorant working overtime and new grass and sun-soaked boy.

I'm awkward, I get it! It's fine, I'm fine, everything's fine.

ANYWAY, once I got my brain back online, I said, "We have to think big. Something unexpected. Something totally original."

Ben shrugged. "I mean, skittles is—"

But before he could finish, Meredith Simmons and

Mindy Liu pranced into our huddle.

"What're you all talking about?" Meredith asked innocently.

The crinkle at the corners of her lips told me she knew exactly what we were talking about. I was fully prepared to ignore her, but Ben said, "Amos wants to put together a proposal for the new exhibit."

Meredith and Mindy did that thing where they have a secret judgmental conversation with just their eyes. Then Meredith turned back to Ben and said, "Well, it's not going to be much of a competition. Mindy and I already have the best idea, and we know it's going to win."

"I mean, it's *really* good," said Mindy. "How could we *not* win?"

As they walked away, I hollered after them, "Daddy's not going to buy you the exhibit, Meredith."

Mom appeared behind us. "What was that?"

"Meredith and Mindy think they have an exhibit proposal that can beat everyone else's," Ben said.

I cringed. It's like he's programmed to automatically respond with the truth. So cute but so naive.

"It'll be up to me and the board to decide that," said Mom. "Everyone will have an equal chance. I take it you three musketeers have something in mind?"

I was about to tell Mom we were going to cook up something good, but Darren Blake, my band teacher (I play percussion), tapped her on the shoulder. He's about Mom's age, and sort of awkward, but a good guy. "Sorry to interrupt, Hannah, but mind if I bother you for a sec?" And there went Mom. Typical. Time for everyone but me.

"You can talk to her when you get home," Chloe said as we walked out of the church. It was still hot and sunny for early evening. She wiggled her eyebrows at us. "Wanna hit a ball around a little before we go? We can think up exhibit ideas while we play."

Ben shook his head. "Dad's gonna be here in a minute."

"Tell him you can't go yet," Chloe said. "You have a surprise shift that you can't miss. Your fellow volunteers are counting on you!"

"I don't think he'll fall for that." Ben laughed. "But I'll see you guys soon."

Not soon enough, I didn't say.

When his cell phone buzzed, Chloe gave Ben a hug goodbye, because that's just something she does, but then I felt like Ben and I should hug, too, and we had this weird moment where our arms both went up and then down and we sort of gave each other a quick side hug like the bros do at school, except we didn't slap each other on the back. His chin came down on my shoulder for half a second. His breath tickled my ear hairs. It was nice. Awkward but nice.

And then he was gone, and Chloe was just staring at me with this big, stupid grin on her face. "Soooooooo?"

"So what?" My cheeks warmed.

"I saw that hug," she said.

"I don't know what you're talking about." I couldn't let her see me blush, so I marched into the grassy field where the cricket equipment was lying out. "Now are we gonna throw the ball around or not?"

"You can deny it." Chloe smirked. "But I see you, Amos Abernathy. Those were some make-out eyes."

"Ew, gross."

"Mm-hmm."

I glanced back at her. "It's not like that. Ben's not—you know, *gay.*"

"How do you know? You ask him?"

"No, but I—"

She laughed. "We'll wait and see." She tapped the side of her nose with her index finger. "Your gay spidey senses might not be tingling, but I've got two eyes and twenty-twenty vision."

I held up two fingers in front of her face. "How many fingers do you see?"

"What?"

"How many fingers do you see?"

"Uh, two?"

I put up two more fingers. "Ooh, sorry. Hate to break it to you, but it doesn't look like your vision's that great after all."

She shoved me, laughing. "Get out of here, Abernathy."

We ended up tossing the cricket ball almost until the sun went down. (You don't catch with a glove in cricket, so I ended up with blisters. I will never understand Chloe's thing with *sports*.) We kept waiting for Mom and Mr. Blake to stop talking, but they went on forever.

I know I told you I'd get to the part about why I'm writing to you, but now my hand is cramping. Tomorrow you'll learn the truth, Albert, I promise.

Your friend,

Amos Abernathy

4

Homestead Exhibit
Saturday, August 13, 2022—9:14 a.m.

As soon as the swarm of kids in matching orange T-shirts tumbles into the cabin, their fingers are on everything. Chloe and I spring into action. Darren must have heard the commotion, because he reappears to help. A freckled white girl a year or two older than me and Chloe elbows between the kids saying, "Hands at your sides. Hands. At. Your. *Sides.*" I recognize the park district's logo on their shirts. Must be a weekend camp.

And just like that, I'm in it. Amos of the twenty-first century evaporates, and I'm a young homesteader from 1851.

I stop a little girl with ivory skin and hay-colored pigtails from knocking over the butter churn I filled with cream earlier. Chloe dances between some kids who ask if she made her shawl herself and if she likes living in a log cabin and if there were always bugs in the house and if and if and if. Between the red-cheeked chaperone, Darren, Chloe, and me, we manage to corral the kids into a clump, coaxing them with promises of the candle-making demonstration.

But a voice stops me before I can start.

"There you are!" My mom, Hannah Abernathy, sweeps in with her vintage, leather-bound notebook, her calico dress *scratching* through the doorway. We have the same pink-white skin that turns reddish brown the further we get into summer. Her brunette hair is done up in a black net. Her crow's-feet claw deep at the corners of her eyes as she squints at Chloe. "Miss Thompson, I fully expected you to be helping Mr. Grimes at the general store. You better get going—there's work to be done!"

Chloe and I know that this is LHP code for, "You're at the wrong station. Get to where you're supposed to be."

"Yes, Miss Abernathy," Chloe mutters, winking out of the log cabin faster than I can say goodbye.

Mom's face softens, her hands flattening the front of her dress. She smiles. "Hello, Mr. Blake."

"Hello, Miss Abernathy."

And this is LHP code for: "Hey, honey."

Ew.

Mom turns to me. "Now, what were you about to show these kind folks, Amos?"

Trying to look annoyed and totally chill at the same time, I rake my hair back with rigid fingers. Then I smile wide, showing off my teeth (I have really good teeth). "I was about to show them how to dip candles." I turn to the group of fidgety kids. "Today we're making *beeswax* candles, but most of the time we make tallow candles. Anyone know what tallow is made of?"

A white chubby boy raises his hand. "Eggshells?"

"No . . . but good try!"

More guesses come without hands.

"Bones?"

"Flowers?"

"Boogers?"

The kids giggle. The chaperone shakes her head. "Tammi, let's keep it appropriate, all right?" The kids laugh harder.

Darren covers up his smirk, and every muscle in my face is trying not to smile. "Those are all great guesses but, actually, tallow is made from melting down animal fat, usually from sheep or cows."

A little Latina girl with light brown skin and thick glasses raises her hand. "How'd they get the fat?"

The chaperone bites her lip, but I give her a reassuring smile—this isn't my first time tiptoeing around the tallow question. "Well, sheep and cows are a main source of food for us pioneers, and we try hard not to let anything go to wa—"

"You mean y-you *kill* them?" Her eyes shimmer. "Just so

you can make a *candle?*"

Oh Lord. "Not just for the candle. Animals are necessary for our survival. Hides are used for clothes, meat for food—"

"But what did they ever do to you?" A tear trickles down her chin.

The chaperone has nearly swallowed her entire lower lip. She glares at me like her laser vision is heating up. Out of the corner of my eye, I catch Mom's arms fold over her chest, fingers squeezing the indents of her elbows.

"Well, we're not using tallow today—this is beeswax, remember, and no bees were hurt to make these candles. They're all very much alive."

"You sure?" The little girl sniffles.

"Positive."

Ten minutes and zero tears later, all the kids have taken a turn dunking the same wick into the beeswax. The sort-of candle it's become is lopsided and dotted with dribbles. Not my best work. I let the girl who cried take it as a souvenir. She's thrilled, and the chaperone thanks me as she shepherds the kids out the back entrance toward the one-room schoolhouse.

Mom sticks around; her fingers lace together in front of her. "Nice save, Amos."

"Oh, thanks." I try to look busy cleaning up the demonstration, hoping she'll leave. The less I see of Mom before three o'clock, the better.

"How're you feeling about today? Ready for the battle this afternoon? Darren says you drummer boys sound better than ever before."

I change tactics and give her a big smile, hoping that will get her to go. "Yeah, I'm fine. *Totally* excited."

Darren's chest puffs. "It's true. Best drummer boys I've ever heard."

Mom smiles at Darren, but when she looks at me, she hesitates. "Amos?"

"Yeah?" I pick up the fire poker and nudge the embers.

Her hand tentatively finds my shoulder, the way you might reach out to find a light switch in the dark. I don't pull away, even though I want to. "Make good decisions today, okay?"

Sweat turns cold on my neck. *What does that mean? Does she know?*

I shrug. "I have to reset for the next group."

And then her hand is gone, and I don't know how I feel. That's the closest we've gotten to a hug, a shoulder squeeze, even a handshake in a while. Maybe I miss things being normal with Mom more than I realize.

"And don't forget to drink a lot of water today," she says on her way out. "Supposed to get up around ninety-five and not much cloud cover. Put on more sunscreen between rotations, too. That goes for both of you gentlemen!"

"As you say, Miss Abernathy." Darren winks.

I say, "All right," but she isn't there to hear my answer.

Darren heads out to tend to the firepit, and I go back to melting more beeswax when an elderly white couple wanders in, holding a map.

Make good decisions today. Mom's words repeat in my head. That almost sounded like an accusation, like she knows about the plan, but she can't know. There's no way.

"Oh, look, Jim," the wrinkled lady says. "It's a little settler boy. Aren't you adorable?"

Jim does not look like he thinks I'm adorable. "What's a man doing inside a log cabin making stew?"

"These are candles, sir."

"Candles? Ain't that women's work?"

I know this type of man. A "simpler times" man. The *worst.*

What I want to say is: "No, Jim. All the womenfolk are hunting and plowing the fields, and I actually enjoy making candles. We smashed the patriarchy out of this log cabin eons ago. We're real progressive pioneers!"

But Mom would kill me.

So I actually say, "Some days I still help Ma around the house. If we want to see anything clearly after sundown, we got to make sure we have a healthy supply of candles. Can I show you how we make them?"

I begin the demonstration, rambling about tallow and

36

beeswax, hating the way Jim walked in judging me. But as I talk, worry pokes at the back of my brain.

Make good decisions today, okay?

What does that mean?

She can't know what's up. If she does, it'll ruin everything.

I need Chloe.

5

Monday, August 16, 2021

Hi, Albert,

Thanks for being patient—today I PROMISE we'll get to why I'm writing to you.

Okay, so, last time on *WHAT IS YOUR LIFE, AMOS?* we saw Chloe shipping me and Ben, and me wondering if Ben is low-key into that idea. So, you know, NO BIG.

Here's the thing. Mom and I live in Apple Grove, Illinois, on the west side of Chickaree County, and most everyone here is cool with LGBTQ+ people. But sometimes I get stares when I wear my pride T-shirt or get overly enthusiastic in public and my hands start flying and my voice squeaks, which happens a lot when it comes to anything about history.

You see, there are two big churches in Apple Grove: there's Grace Hill, which is super welcoming and open-minded (that's where Mom and I go), and then there's Holy Cross. Last summer this high school senior Jessica, whose family goes to Holy Cross, came out as a lesbian. Then Gareth Gunner, the pastor at Holy Cross, refused to let Jessica take Communion until she agreed to have pastoral counseling sessions with him to "discuss her life choices."

Albert, as you are aware, being queer is not a choice. It's who we are. Period.

Now that she's out of high school, Jessica comes to Grace Hill. She's on the worship team and dating Trish, who plays bass on the worship team, and she's figuring out what to do with her family, but the point of all of this . . . is that Ben's family goes to Holy Cross.

The only time I've really had a conversation with Ben's parents was when they visited the LHP this past April, a month after Ben started volunteering.

Ben, Chloe, and I were setting up a game of cricket in the field by the fort. His parents waved to us, and a change came over Ben. It was like his shoulders and arms turned to wood.

"What are you doing here?" Ben asked as they walked up to us.

"Oh, honey," said Mrs. Oglevie. "We wanted to surprise you! I can't believe it's taken us this long to see you all dressed up." She flattened the collar of his shirt. "Just precious, all of you."

"You kids look the spitting image of *Little House on the Prairie*," Mr. Oglevie said. He has these permanently angry eyebrows. (I bet a pair of tweezers could fix that right up.) He turned to me and Chloe. "We're Ben's parents."

"Nice to meet you," Chloe and I said together.

Mrs. Oglevie fiddled with the silver cross hanging around her pale neck. "Who are your friends, Ben?"

"This is Chloe and, um, Amos."

Have you ever seen a chameleon change color, Albert? It's insanely fast. That's how quickly Mr. and Mrs. Oglevie's smiles fell when Ben said my name. They didn't change color, of course. But their expressions sure did. And the tension in their muscles. The straightness of their spines.

Mrs. Oglevie was the first to recover. "Chloe. And Amos. We—we've heard so much about you. Both of you." Her eyes roved over me like she had X-ray vision and was trying to see what was under my skin.

Mr. Oglevie stared at me. "Ben mentioned you go to Grace Hill. I told him he should invite you both to a Wednesday night at Holy Cross. The Lord has been working miracles of transformation midweek for months now. We'd love to see you there."

Everyone knows Wednesday nights are "new believer" nights at all the local churches. "Thanks, but we're pretty happy at Grace Hill," I said.

"Maybe you could come with us some time, Ben," Chloe said.

Ben's eyes darted from Chloe to me to his parents,

who'd gone even more rigid than before. "I don't—"

Mrs. Oglevie interrupted Ben. "You're sweet to offer, but we're dedicated Holy Crossers. All us Oglevies are there every Sunday, rain, shine, or otherwise."

Ben's jaw clamped tight.

Mr. Oglevie shifted his weight from one foot to the other. "We should let the kids get back to work, hon. Nice to meet you both."

"Find us at the end of your shift, Ben," Mrs. Oglevie said. "We'll wander around until you're done. So good to finally put faces to names, Chloe. And Amos."

As soon as they were out of earshot, I said, "Sooooo, that was awkward. What did you tell your parents about us?"

Ben scratched the back of his head. "Nothing. I don't know."

"You clearly told them *something*," Chloe said. "They acted like we were devil children." She laughed.

I didn't laugh, because I suddenly realized what he could have told them to make them act that way. "You told them I was gay, didn't you?"

Ben hesitated. "I mean, I tell my parents everything. And they—well, they've got strong opinions, is all."

Chloe picked up a cricket bat, swinging it through the air. "You mean, they're homophobic?"

Ben's forehead wrinkled. "That's not what I said."

41

"You didn't have to," I told him.

You see how this is getting complicated, Albert, right?

Now, fast-forward again to two days ago, this past Saturday, at the LHP, when Ben and I were walking to meet Chloe at the schoolhouse.

Ben was trying to convince me that Andrew Garfield is the best Spider-Man. I argued there's no competition when it comes to Tom Holland. (Sorry, Tobey Maguire.) Ben was about to come back at me when he stopped short.

I turned around. "Giving up that easily?"

But Ben wasn't paying attention to me. He was watching two men, one white and the other Black with dark brown skin, walking across the park over by the old general store. They were holding hands.

I wouldn't say gay couples are common in Chickaree County, but they aren't unheard of. I couldn't tell if he was curious or anxious or being rude because they were an interracial couple, but whatever he was feeling, he was staring at them like he'd spotted a two-headed unicorn. And that wasn't cool. "Um, earth to Ben!"

"What?" He didn't even turn to look at me.

"Why are you staring at that gay couple?" There was an edge to my voice. After meeting his parents, I wondered just how judgmental he might really be.

He quickly looked at me and blushed. "I'm not. I just—I thought I saw something."

Suuuuure. I raised an eyebrow. "Yeah, a gay couple?"

Ben's cheeks reddened even more, but he still wouldn't look me in the eye. "Can I ask you something?"

My heart pounded faster than it should have. "Sure."

"Do you think . . ." His eyes drifted back to the gay men. "Do you think gay people would have belonged here?"

I don't know what I was expecting, but it definitely wasn't that! "What?"

He looked out over the grounds, and my eyes followed his, searching the other groups of volunteers at the blacksmith, the printshop, the Wakefield House. The pairs of men and women, boys and girls. I watched his eyes taking it all in. They glinted almost green for a moment.

"You know," he said quietly. "Boys who . . . liked boys. Or girls who liked girls. Or whatever. Did they exist back then?"

At first, I was, like, OF COURSE GAY PEOPLE EXISTED, but when I tried to think of a queer person from the nineteenth century, my mind went blank. "I—I'm not sure. I guess I've never really thought about it like that."

Then he looked at me. "Do you ever feel like you just don't belong? Like you're a penny that got stuck with a bunch of quarters?"

Now I was getting offended. "Wait—what? Are you saying I'm not worth as much as everyone else?"

"No, no!" Ben waved his hands at me. "That's not what I meant. I meant being *different*."

43

"Being gay doesn't make me *that* different. I'm still a *person*. I've *always* belonged, here and everywhere, just like everyone else. It doesn't matter if I like boys." But I paused. I couldn't shake the fact that I had never learned any history, especially from the nineteenth century, about queer people. Definitely not in any social studies class. And, really, I hadn't even *thought* much about it. All of a sudden I wasn't mad at Ben. I was mad at myself, embarrassed that the question had never even occurred to me, an *actual* gay person. I looked at him sheepishly. "But . . . that is a good question. Where *is* the history of queer people? Like, *before* 1960? Were there queer settlers here? Soldiers? Farmers?"

Ben shrugged. He was looking more uncomfortable by the second.

His discomfort must have been contagious. I looked around at what I'd always thought of as a second home, and all I saw, as far as I could tell, were straight, cisgender people. No one else here was like me. Definitely none of the volunteers, at least. And even though I know we're all technically *acting*, it was suddenly like I was acting at *acting*. A double imposter. I got queasy, wondering what people thought when they saw me, talked with me. Had I always reenacted like I am a straight cis boy instead of a *gay* cis boy? The more I thought about it, the more I realized how much I've always acted straight at the LHP because, for some reason, my brain wouldn't let me be *me*. As if that was inauthentic. As if *I* couldn't be authentic.

I felt like I'd shrunk. I felt so small. For the first time in my life, I felt like maybe this place, this history, this world—my home—didn't belong to me. Not the LHP or Apple Grove or Illinois. It was like I'd been thinking I was a tree all my life, knowing my roots linked me to the past, only to discover that I was just a trunk and leaves. No roots. No connections. No past.

I knew right then what I needed to do. "I'm going to find them."

Ben turned back to me. "Who?"

"The queers."

"What?"

I said, "I'm going to find the history of queer people in the nineteenth century. I—"

"Maybe not so loud, Amos?"

"No one's listening."

He craned his head around, double- and triple-checking that no one was paying attention to us. "You really think you'll find anything?"

"I'm Amos Abernathy, son of Hannah Abernathy, Queen of History—of course I will." I smiled. "People like me didn't just sprout from the ground in the last hundred years. Someone queer *must* have lived here."

He laughed nervously. "Right."

"I'm usually right." I paused, suddenly struck by the most brilliant idea ever. "Oh my god, Ben. That's it!"

"What's it?"

I grabbed his arm. "Come on. We need to find Chloe."

She was standing outside the schoolhouse, chewing on an apple. Between gasps, I said, "I know what we're going to do for our exhibit proposal! Listen to this: 'Forgotten Voices: LGBTQ+ Stories of the Nineteenth Century.' Or something like that. What do you think?"

Chloe nodded slowly. "I mean, it's not cricket or black-smithing, but, yeah, that might be cool." Then she leaned in closer. "No offense, Amos, but, like, *were* there gay people back then?"

"That's my *point*!"

Ben looked less convinced. As soon as I said "LGBTQ+," he peeked over his shoulder again like I'd cursed. "I don't know if Chickaree County is . . . uh . . . ready for something like that."

I grabbed each of them by a shoulder. Even through his shirt, the heat of Ben's skin lit up some unknown part of my brain like a firefly; Albert, it drives me bananas that I can't even touch him without getting googly-eyed. "That's exactly *why* we need to do it," I said. "Queer folks *must* exist in history. I mean, I *know* they do. But like *American* history, during the Civil War. And *here*, in Illinois. But I can't think of any! I bet people have just been ignoring us all this time."

46

"It *would* be something no one else is doing," Chloe mused. "And I bet an exhibit like that would really put the Living History Park on the map, you know? Like, show the rest of the world how progressive the semirural Midwest can be."

Ben's forehead wrinkled. "But the semirural Midwest *isn't* all that progressive. At least not the parts I know. Not everyone's parents are like yours, you guys."

I looked him square in the eye and said, "This is my chance to show the world I belong here, and that I belonged back then. We can prove that queer people have *always* belonged. We just don't get the spotlight like we should."

I couldn't help but wonder, or hope, really, if by "I belong here" I meant "We belong here." Me and Ben. (*I just mean you have a nice face.*) His lips twitched, but he wasn't blushing anymore.

I just don't know how to read him sometimes.

That didn't mean I was going to let his bad attitude stop me. As soon as I got home, I googled "19th century queer people."

All I got at first was a lot of LGBTQ+ history from Europe, which was irritating. (I mean, great for Europe, but . . .) There *was* one article about a couple of women in Vermont in a partnership, but I couldn't find much else. And that wasn't *here*. It's no wonder my GSA friends are always talking about getting out of Illinois when they're older. Sure, Chicago is great, but they go on and on about how places like New York or California would be "so much better." But this is *home*. I love Illinois. I love Chickaree County and Apple Grove. Maybe not feeling connected to our history is part of *why* my friends want to leave. Maybe that's why none of them ever want to volunteer! Deep down they feel like they *can't* belong.

That makes me so sad, Albert.

So I needed to find someone queer close to home. There was no other option. Finding a queer ancestor could change my friends' lives. It could change my life. And maybe Ben's. So I added "Illinois" to my search.

And *that's* how I found you, Albert. When I read your name, I legit almost cried. This might sound corny, but I mean it; it was like God actually heard me. Like that feeling I had in New Hope Church when Mom announced the call for exhibit proposals was leading me to you. You are the ONLY person listed under the "Nineteenth Century" heading in the Wikipedia article "LGBT history in Illinois." (Don't worry, I didn't stop at Wikipedia—it was just the first thing that came up.) Since then, I've been learning everything I can about you.

You were assigned female at birth in Ireland on Christmas Day, 1843. When you were a teenager, around the time the Civil War started, you immigrated to America, to Belvidere, Illinois, which is only a couple of hours away from me. You changed your name to Albert D. J. Cashier (I'm not going to write your birth name—I know deadnaming isn't cool). Then you enlisted in the Union army as a man. You were eighteen when you did that. Only like five years older than me. I can't even start to imagine *actually* going to war, and *you* fought for THREE WHOLE YEARS. And one of the coolest things? After the Civil War you moved to Saunemin, which is only a couple of towns over! We are practically neighbors! OH MY GOD!

So, I know that a lot of women dressed up as men so they could fight in the Civil War, but that wasn't your story. You were Albert before you enlisted, you were Albert after the war was over, and you were Albert until you died in 1915. Even though the words didn't exist back then, today I'm pretty sure you'd be a trans man.

I know we don't share the same identity, but we share Illinois and being in the queer community. I don't know if you liked boys or girls or just people or maybe you didn't feel romantic about anyone at all (you never got married), but I know your pronouns, your name, and how you presented yourself. My GSA friends all identify differently from me, too, but queer pride, our stories and our struggles and our victories, that's what connects us, and we're stronger because of it. And when we're all there for each other, when we work together, it's harder for ignorant people to hate or ignore or forget us.

Knowing you existed makes me feel like I have roots again. Or maybe for the first time ever. I can't believe that I've lived in Illinois my whole life, in a town SO CLOSE to where you lived, and I didn't learn about you until today. That's messed up.

Now I'm wondering who else my teachers and the history books haven't told me about. If you existed in the nineteenth century, there's got to be more proof that someone or *many* queer someones did, too. Maybe there's all this queer history heteronormative-obsessed adults have been keeping under wraps, out of schools and textbooks and common knowledge.

That's why I'm writing you this letter. Albert, we're going to find them. Together, we're going to prove to Ben and Mr. and Mrs. Oglevie and everyone else that queer people belonged in the past and that we belong here now.

And maybe, when we do, I'll figure out if Ben likes my face or if he *like*-likes my face.

That stays between us.

Thanks, Albert.

Your friend,

Amos Abernathy

6

Tulane General Store
Saturday, August 13, 2022—9:47 a.m.

I duck out of the homestead as soon as I see Jill Maldonado and Melissa Clipper walking down the path.

"Sorry, gotta go," I holler over my shoulder, haversack clanking against my thigh. "Beeswax is ready by the fire and there's more cubes on the shelf if you need them. And Mr. Blake's out back."

Melissa asks something about the butter churn, but I'm already speeding away. Getting to Chloe is way more important than pre-butter.

Morning sun cuts sharp into my eyes as I run-walk past the printshop and post office. The park is buzzing with families, some in modern clothes and a few enthusiastic folks dressed for the 1860s, in everything from fancy dresses to farmhand overalls. I don't pay any attention to their raised eyebrows as I dodge strollers and hoopskirts.

On any other Saturday, the LHP would be lucky to see

even half this many visitors. People travel from all over to be a part of the celebration. The hardcore Civil War interpreters, who seriously stan reenacting, camp out in canvas tents along Mulberry Creek for the entire week. Don't get me wrong, I'm committed, but even *I* have my limits. Indoor plumbing is a must.

I sidestep a toddler gnawing on a stick of purple rock candy and make my way to Tulane General Store. The muted gray building has a wide front porch with a line of rocking chairs. An older Latina woman sits in one with a child on her lap, fanning herself with an informational brochure.

Chloe looks up from the uneven slats of the porch as I bound up the steps, huffing for breath. She's kneeling in front of a chalkboard sign where she's writing the daily discount in perfect cursive.

"What's going on?" she asks, dusting her chalky gray hands on her dress as she stands. The woman in the rocking chair and her child eye us strangely. A young white couple following up the steps behind me watch us like we're mascots at a theme park about to break into song. When I shoot them a look, they take off toward the glass bowls of penny candy and racks of T-shirts and hoodies.

"My mom," I say, "I think she knows."

Chloe is back to inspecting her chalk art. "Knows what?"

"About this afternoon—our *three o'clock* plans?" I stare

her down. "*You* didn't say anything to her, did you?"

Her chin pulls back defensively. "And why would I do that?"

"I don't know. Maybe you got nervous or decided it's not worth it or—"

Her finger flies to my lips. "Amos, I *didn't* say anything. You know that. We're in this together, no matter what." Chloe side-eyes a couple of pasty boys about our age, snickering over a cell phone. "Why do you think she knows?"

"She was being weird at the homestead, after you left," I say. "Said I should 'make good decisions' today. The way she said it—it was like she was really saying 'I know what you're planning, and don't you dare.'"

"You're reading into it way too much. Maybe she's just worried since it's the first day of CWRW."

I sit on the stoop. "No, it was more than that."

"Amos, you're nervous, I get it. I won't blame you if you don't want to go through with—"

"That's not it at all. But I'm telling you, something is off."

A sweet voice turns my mood even more sour. "Well, look who it is! She-Ra and She-Hulk. What a fine day, don't you think?"

My teeth grind together.

Meredith Simmons stands on the dirt path in a freshly pressed blue checkered dress. Her chestnut hair is curled into sausage ringlets on the sides and back, parted neatly along the top. A gleam flashes in her blue eyes, and I know she's up to no good. In her left hand is a large wooden ring that looks like a hula hoop prototype. In her right hand she holds a short wooden stick. She must have wandered off from the Wakefield House, where volunteers demonstrate games kids used to play.

"Don't you have someone else's day to ruin, Meredith?" I ask.

"Where are your manners, Amos Abernathy?" she chides, her voice in full-on character mode; a little twangy, a twist of Southern belle rounding out the edges of each word. My own personal nails on a chalkboard.

"My manners are just fine, *Meredith Simmons*," I say. "Go on and torture someone else."

"And you can take your microaggressions with you," Chloe adds.

Meredith ignores Chloe, only proving her point, and a grin slides onto her face. She really can make awful look innocent. A couple passes by, and Meredith says, louder than before, "Oh, Amos, aren't you excited about the celebration going on? And you know what the pride and joy of this year's Civil War Remembrance Week is? That *inspired* new exhibit. You've seen it, of course?"

My fingernails bite into my palms, but Chloe's hand wraps around my arm, forcing me to stay in place.

"*Of course* we have, Meredith." She marches down to the bottom step and stops, towering over Meredith McAwful. I can hear the forced smile in Chloe's voice. "The whole town's been simply *buzzing* with joy!"

Meredith's smile drops. Even *she* knows when she's being mocked. "Don't say it like that!"

Chloe pouts exaggeratedly. "Don't go being offended now. Come on, let's play."

Without a second's hesitation, Chloe tugs the hoop from Meredith's hand and hurls it down the path like an old tire. It rolls through a group of visitors, who watch it barrel by with curious glances.

"Hey!" Meredith yips.

Chloe smiles widely. "Don't tell me you aren't willing to play nice now! Go on after it, Meredith Simmons!"

I stifle a laugh.

Meredith holds Chloe's gaze, her baby blues hiding that cool flame I know is underneath. "Daddy's gonna hear about this. You're bullying me!"

"I hope he does. Tell him we had a *lovely* time together."

The muscles in Meredith's jaw contract. "And *I* hope you enjoy your apprenticeship while it lasts." She stomps off.

"Well, wasn't that nice!" Chloe hikes up her dress and sits down next to me. She drops the overly cheery tone. "I'm sure I'm going to get an earful for telling her off. She's probably already halfway to Daddy."

"Chloe, I appreciate you standing up for me, but you didn't have to do that," I say. "You're already risking too much by helping me this afternoon. If you lose your—"

"For the last time, I know what I'm risking," Chloe says. "And I believe it's worth the risk. No matter what."

"Thanks." I lean into her. "I wish Meredith Simmons— *all* the Simmonses—would just disappear."

Chloe rolls her eyes at me. "What else is new?"

It's actually because of Meredith Simmons that Chloe and I became friends. In fourth grade I told Meredith I was gay. She was my library buddy and we'd been pretty close all year. One day she told me that this other girl, Sarah, liked me and Meredith wanted to know if I liked her back. I should have lied, but I thought I could trust her, so I told Meredith the truth. Then she told the whole class my secret. There were jokes. Some kids started saying I had "gay germs" and that touching me would make them gay, too. For a whole week I ate lunch alone.

And then one day, Chloe came up to me in the cafeteria. "My mom's best friend is gay," she'd said, the way other people might say "The sky is blue." She sat down and asked, "What kind of chips do you have today?"

I eyed the kids snickering across the cafeteria. "You sure you want to eat with me? They'll make fun of you."

"Let them. Chloe Thompson does not have time for

mean kids," she said.

We've been inseparable ever since. And Meredith Simmons has only gotten worse.

A warm gust blows over us and the absolute worst possibility hits me. "You don't think *she* knows, do you?"

Chloe fiddles with her shawl. "How would Meredith know anything?"

"She has her ways. Spies everywhere—I bet her family's got half the town working for them."

"*Oooookay*. Settle down." Her shoulder digs into mine.

I pause, kind of losing myself in a daydream where I tell Meredith all the things I'd really like to say. When Chloe sniffs loudly, I come back to reality. "I wouldn't have *actually* punched her, you know," I clarify.

"Mm-hmm."

The group of white kids stumbles out of the general store. We scoot off the steps to avoid being trampled.

"Sheesh!" Chloe says. "We *like* history. We don't want to *be* history!"

The boys just laugh and wander off.

"Boys can be so annoying," I grumble. Of course, I'm thinking about Ben again. I sling my haversack over my head. "Where are you headed next?"

"Homestead. You?"

"Wakefield House."

"Cool. I'll see you at the schoolhouse after." Chloe

catches my wrist before I can leave. "Amos, everything's going to be fine this afternoon. I really believe that. Actually, no. Everything's going to be *great*! Don't stress. Okay?"

I nod quickly. "Okay."

She smiles, and we head in opposite directions. A knot pulls tight in my stomach. What if everything isn't fine? Chloe and I, we'll lose all of this, and it'll be all my fault. Then I hear Chloe's voice from behind me. "Hey, Abernathy! What kind of chips you got today?"

The knot loosens. I can't help but smile. Without looking back, I shout, "You'll have to wait and see!"

7

Sunday, August 22, 2021

Dear Albert,

I thought I knew a lot about the Civil War. I mean, I spend pretty much all my spare time pretending to live in the 1800s. But learning about you has sent me down a rabbit hole of nineteenth-century history I've never even heard about, and not just queer history. Things they didn't teach us in school about slavery. How Black people weren't really free after the war ended. About the Reconstruction era. About the Dred Scott court case.

Albert, did you know Free Frank McWorter? Apparently, he was the first African American to ever found a town in the United States, and he did it right here in Illinois in 1836! I mean, that's like MAJOR history, once again from my home state, that I haven't learned about.

It hit me while I was reading about Free Frank McWorter that all the LGBTQ+ research I've done so far has focused on *white* queer people. I can't believe I was doing that, even subconsciously. Queer history isn't about one race, it's about *all* races. So I've started researching BIPOC LGBTQ+ nineteenth-century American history specifically, and that information is just as hard to find, if not harder. The most interesting story I've come across so far is about Addie Brown and Rebecca Primus, two free Black women from the mid-1800s who had a VERY close friendship.

The more research I do, the more I realize that when I think of the Living History Park, my mind almost entirely goes to the history of white people. I know there are some photos and plaques in the gallery at the LHP about slavery and the rights of African Americans, but we almost never talk about race. Only Lincoln signing the Emancipation Proclamation or how much "better" things were for African Americans toward the end of the 1800s. Why are we ignoring so much history? Because it's awful? Because it hurts to talk about?

And then I think about Chloe. If we really were reenacting "authentic history," she would probably have been enslaved. Even in Illinois! Did you know Illinois was a free state by 1818, but white people were still able to own slaves who worked in salt mines? How is that FREE?!

And that makes me wonder: If Chloe wouldn't have been free, why would she even want to volunteer? I mean, I know why she did, but . . . *why?*

She started in fifth grade after Cadence, her sister who's

eight years older, went to college. Chloe felt kind of low without her, so her grandma Justine, who had volunteered here with the quilters club, suggested Chloe join me as a junior volunteer. But in all this time we've never talked about how she feels about being a Black person reenacting a life that is historically inaccurate. It's like I was saying before—we're playing pretend *pretend*.

And now I'm thinking about Mindy Liu, who is Chinese American, and Jill Maldonado, who's Mexican and Filipina. I've always acted like we all would have been treated the same during the 1800s, but that's just not true, and no one I know at the LHP has ever talked about it. Don't get me wrong, Albert. I love that the park is inclusive, but not talking about *all* of history . . . that doesn't sit right.

I don't know why we don't learn or talk about this stuff. If I'm being honest, we need a whole bunch of new exhibits at the LHP to cover all the history we're missing. If I could write a hundred proposals, I would, and maybe I will someday, but for now, I want to tell your story because it feels like *our* story. I mean, *you're from Illinois*. Even though we don't identify the same way, we're both from the queer community. You're my roots. I was meant to find you. (Or maybe you found me? I don't know. Maybe that's weird.) THE POINT IS that yesterday I told Ben and Chloe about all of my research, but I was most excited to tell them about you.

We were stationed at the Wakefield House. Ben and Chloe were dueling tops.

"You guys will never believe who I found," I said. "A transgender Civil War hero! Well, *probably* transgender."

"Get out," said Chloe. Ben was quiet. The tops bumped into each other, but they kept spinning.

"For real." I pulled out this journal, where I've also been keeping notes about you and everything else I find. "His name was Albert D. J. Cashier and he served in the Ninety-Fifth Illinois Infantry. He fought for three years, and when the war was over, he moved to Saunemin."

The tops wobbled.

"Whoa," said Chloe. "That's like eerily close to here."

"I know!"

Ben said, "Okay, but how do you know this 'Albert' was actually, uh, transgender? I've read about women who dressed up as men to fight in the war. They did it for all sorts of reasons. To find their missing husbands, to earn decent money, the chance to fight. That doesn't make them, you know . . ."

I guess I shouldn't have been surprised by Ben's response, but it still bugged me. "Albert used he/him pronouns before, during, and after the war. He used them until he died. Even his gravestone says Albert. It's not like I can call him up and ask him"—BUT OMG ALBERT THAT WOULD MAKE MY LIFE—"but all signs point to him being a queero."

62

Queero = queer + hero. Obviously, you deserve the title.

ANYWAY, Ben picked up his fallen top, which had gotten knocked down by Chloe's. "Weren't you just talking the other day about how people shouldn't assume other people's identities?"

I sighed. "I meant that people shouldn't assume everyone is straight and cisgender."

Ben huffed. "Seems a little hypocritical to me." He dropped his top back onto the wood porch, where it spun almost perfectly in place.

Ben might be cute, but that doesn't mean I won't fight with him when he's wrong. Fortunately for him, Chloe leaned in and asked, "What else did you find about Albert?" Then she spun her top and it whizzed next to Ben's.

"Let's see." I flipped through my notes. "Um, well, Albert had a whole bunch of odd jobs after the war. He was a cemetery worker for a while."

"Creepy," said Chloe, "but kind of awesome. Doesn't sound like Albert was afraid of much—first a war and then a graveyard? Eek."

I nodded. "Not to mention that it was still the queer dark ages."

Ben finally nodded in agreement, but his tone was still kind of defensive. "*Fine*, Albert was brave. Totally get that. I mean, women caught pretending to be soldiers were jailed or worse. But is it really worth it if you're risking so much?"

"But Albert wasn't pretending," I said. "That's important for people to know. He was a man." I took a deep breath. "And since Albert made Illinois his home and he's *practically* our neighbor, it only makes sense that he should be the star of our exhibit proposal. We owe it to him. What do you think?"

Chloe said, "You know I'm in."

"Ben?"

"I don't know. . . ."

"Dude, come on." I groaned. I couldn't believe he was backing down. "You're the one who inspired this whole proposal! If you hadn't asked that question about that ga—"

Ben grabbed his haversack. "I need some water."

Chloe and I watched him dart into the sunlight.

"What's his deal?" she said.

All I could think was: *You have a nice face.*

You have a nice face.

You have a nice face.

"I think—" My insides were getting all wormy again. Maybe Ben was worried about what he would be risking if he said yes to working with us. Because what if there *was* something big Ben was going to risk his parents finding out about? He could be gay, right? So, I shoved off the porch. "I think I need to talk to him."

Chloe called after me, "Amos—"

"I'll be right back." I waved her off. I could tell by her huff that she was getting irritated with me, but I had to get this weirdness figured out with Ben.

It was even hotter out of the shade than I thought it would be. I hustled down the path and around the corner. Ben was at one of the public water fountains. He was filling his tin cup, watching the water go in like it had offended him.

"Ben, hey," I said.

The tin cup almost slipped from his hand. "Amos. I said I'd be right back."

"I know." It was so bright, I had to create a visor with my fingers. "But I wanted to talk. I feel like ever since that, uh, conversation we had, about our, um, faces, things have been different between us. I just wanted to say that I'm sorry if I made you feel uncomfortable. I didn't mean—"

He let go of the spigot and pulled away from the fountain. The tin cup rested in his hands the way you might hold a baby chick. He said, "What? Oh. No, Amos, you don't have to apologize. I—I just . . ."

I just *knew* he was trying to say he wasn't gay—but he couldn't even get the words out! Like they were dirty or something. That hurt more than I expected. So I let him off the hook and finished for him. "You just aren't like me. Like, into dudes, I mean."

Ben's ears turned crimson. And then for some reason *my* ears started burning and we both ended up looking at our toes.

His finger tapped the side of his cup. "Amos, I shouldn't have said what I said."

I freaking hate how my heart hiccupped. "So . . . you don't like my face, then?"

The cup shook in his hands. "That's not what I'm saying."

"Then what *are* you saying?" Of course my voice just *had* to crack when I said that.

"Why do you have to be so difficult?" he snapped. Water sloshed over the side of his cup. "Why can't I just say that I like your face? Why does that have to make me something? Why can't I be me, just Ben, and like your face? Why do you have to give words to everything? Maybe Albert was just a woman who really, really liked dressing up like a man. And maybe I just like your face! Okay?"

It was like I'd walked into a wall of wind. How could he say that about you, Albert? I showed him the evidence. It was like he didn't trust me. I couldn't understand why he was in such denial about *everything*.

Well, except about liking my face.

He still liked my face.

And, in the moment, that thought stomped out all of my other questions.

I couldn't help my mouth turning into a ridiculous grin.

66

"So, you *do* like my face, then?"

I half expected Ben to smash his cup on the ground and stomp off, but he didn't. His lips twitched like he couldn't control them, and then he was smiling, too.

Then I didn't know what to think. I started to get really hot. Heavy-in-my-chest hot.

"I'm not saying anything else." Ben dodged around me. "C'mon. Let's get back. Don't think I put enough sunscreen on this morning."

My heart skipped. And then I literally skipped after him. (Albert, SKIPPING? What is this boy doing to me?)

When we got back to Chloe, it was like nothing had happened at all, which was sort of infuriating. Ben went right back to playing tops with Chloe, and I joined in, because what else was I supposed to do?

Albert, I've given this a LOT of thought. Like, I legit can't stop thinking about what happened with Ben. And you know what? I've decided that some people are really good at saying things by not saying anything at all, and I'm pretty sure that's what Ben did. He didn't say the words outright, but by not saying it, I think he was *trying* to tell me that he *does* like me. That maybe he *is* gay, and I haven't been losing my mind thinking he's just saying words to make me think he is!

I've been calling myself gay for years now. Sometimes I forget how even I had to really chew the word like an old stick of gum before it came out right. And even though I knew it wouldn't be a big deal for Mom, I still remember the heaviness I felt before I told her. Like I'd been carrying around stones all my life and I hadn't known it. But when I told Mom I was gay, she just hugged me and told me she loved me, and the stones broke up into tiny bits of gravel.

Sometimes I still feel them rumbling around when I have to tell someone I'm not straight, because, you know, *straight's the default*. UGH. But I can always go back to how Mom reacted. She was good about that, even if she's not always great about other things.

Now I'm thinking about how Ben's parents would react if he told them he's gay. Not like Mom, that's for sure. And I'm thinking about Jessica and Holy Cross and Mr. and Mrs. Oglevie wanting Chloe and me to go to a Wednesday night group. . . .

Nope. None of that gives me a good feeling. And I want nothing but good feelings for Ben.

Albert, maybe Ben needs this exhibit proposal project just as much as I do. (If what I think he's thinking is true.) Maybe he needs it even *more* than me. If he can see himself in the past, find his roots, call himself what he is with pride, maybe then it won't be so bad for him. Maybe he'll be able to just be himself.

No more stones.

Then he can tell everyone that he thinks I have a nice face.

That would be cool.

Talk soon,

Amos Abernathy

8

Wakefield House
Saturday, August 13, 2022—10:01 a.m.

There's a small crowd gathered around the porch at the Wakefield House. A group of fourth- and fifth-grade junior volunteers are tossing beanbags and spinning tops. I'm sitting on the wide porch next to Andrea Dominguez, who is darning a wool sock, probably one she knitted herself. Today she's wearing a red-checked dress. Her almost black hair is in a braid down her back, and her olive skin has gotten at least two shades darker from so much time in the sun. She's going into eighth grade and she's *super* into yarn.

"What's going on with you?" she asks, fingers and needle tucking and turning robotically.

Clearly, I'm failing at not looking worried. I scoop up a Jacob's ladder and flip the top square of wood. The lower squares, connected by strands of red ribbon, jump and flip like a wriggling snake. "It's nothing."

"Doesn't look like nothing."

I go with a half-truth. "Guess I'm just nervous about this afternoon."

"The battle? You'll be fine—this is what, like, your millionth year being a reenactor?" She laughs.

I say, "Ha ha, yeah. Right."

"Really," Andrea says, fingers and needle coming to stop. "You and the guys are great. Mr. Blake won't stop talking about how awesome you all sound in practice."

I shake my head like there's water clogging my ears. "You're right." A deep breath, a flash of smile. "Everything's going to be great."

Andrea goes back to her sock, humming quietly to herself. I let my fake smile fall.

A couple of white fourth-grade volunteers I haven't learned the names of walk by on stilts, which are just these simple eight-foot-long two-by-four beams of wood cut vertically with little wedges nailed at the bottom. Kids only stand a few extra inches off the ground, but there's still a trick to balancing. The uneven cobblestoned street in front of the house makes it especially hard to walk without falling off the stilts. I secretly/not-so-secretly love when cocky visitors think they'll be able to use them on their first try.

Sure enough, it's not long before a bunch of curious visitors are trying them out. I have to turn my head away to laugh when a white kid wearing a band T-shirt and athletic shorts totally wipes out after two steps. Andrea and I cough to cover up our laughter as he tumbles two, three, four more times before giving up with a "whatever."

One of the LHP kids, a tanned, almost sunburned white girl with braces, skips up to the porch. "You're Amos, right?"

"Last time I checked. What's your name?"

"Madison."

"Nice to meet you, Madison."

She pulls a folded-up piece of notebook paper out of her dress pocket. "This is for you. I didn't read it, I promise."

Suuuuure, I totally believe you. I take the note from her. She skips away, picks up a pair of stilts, and shows off her skills to a new gaggle of passersby. She's not half bad.

The paper is slightly damp. Ew. Fourth-grade sweat.

Sweat aside, this is weird. I can't remember the last time someone wrote me an actual note. The handwriting is kind of familiar, though, the way the letters of my name sort of slant to the right, but I can't place where I've seen it before. I unfold the note.

A hummingbird takes flight in my chest.

Amos,

I got your text. Tried texting you back this morning, but I realized you wouldn't have your phone on you at the LHP. I want to talk. I know you have big plans for

*today, but it's important. If you're willing to talk, give
this note to Chloe.*

Ben

I read it two more times, and now *my* palms are sweating through the thin paper.

Ben. No freaking way.

My trembling fingers tuck the note into my haversack.

"What's up with that?" Andrea asks.

I jump—almost forgot she was sitting there. "It's nothing."

She cocks her head skeptically. "You sure have a whole lot of nothing going on today."

"It's fine." I shove myself off the porch. Madison has made her way down the cobblestoned road at the opposite end of the Wakefield House. I jog to her.

"Who gave you that note?"

She shrugs. "Some boy."

"What did he look like?"

"Like a *boy*, I don't know." She maneuvers around me, agile as a spider. "But he looked kind of familiar. And he knew how to play skittles."

Ben really was here.

"We were going to play," Madison goes on, "but then he said he had to go."

"Did you see where he went?"

"Nope."

"That's all you remember? He didn't say anything else?"

"That's right." Madison stilts back to her friends, and I overhear her say, "Boys are so weird." They giggle.

But this isn't a joke. Ben's here. Ben's *here*. I wanted Ben here, didn't I? Freaking Ben Oglevie. Do I want to talk to him? I don't think I want to talk to him anymore. But I have to talk to him. What am I thinking? Of course, I want to talk to him! I'm not talking to him. What's he going to say? What if he only makes it worse? I can't do worse. I'm already worse. I'm not going to—

A woman's voice cuts through my panic. "What can you tell us about this?" She's standing next to the skittles board with two ruddy boys, probably no older than seven.

It takes me a moment to remember I'm still on the job. This woman and her children expect me to be in character. Another deep breath. Another smile. "I was just about to get a game of skittles going. Want to learn how to play?"

I rattle off the rules as we hover over the skittles board, but now Ben's jammed in my brain again. All I can picture is how his face lit up the first time I showed him the open-top, rectangular wood box, the different "rooms" in which players set up nine pins, or skittles. The object of the game is to spin a top from one end of the board to the other, knocking down as many skittles as you can. The skittles closer to the front are worth fewer points than the three in the back. I was the skittles champion until Ben showed up.

The boys take turns winding the string around the top, pulling it like a rip cord on a parachute, and sending it spinning down the alley. The younger brother knocks down two pins on his first go, but the older brother manages to get the top into the far-left corner, knocking down a pin worth one hundred points.

"You two are naturals." I beam. "My friend Ben, he made up some extra rules and built his own boards with new designs and specialized tops."

The mom's eyebrows rise, impressed. "So, kids really *could* find something to do with their time before video games, huh?"

The brothers groan. *"Mom!"*

She chuckles, ushering them off with a hand on each of their backs. She turns her head to me. "Thanks for showing them how to play."

I wave goodbye and set the board up again. A pasty, sunscreen-slathered middle-aged couple who were watching from a distance ask to play. I go over the rules again and then retreat to the shady porch. I haven't even spent fifteen minutes in the sun and my pants are already sticking to my thighs. I tug the front of my shirt, forcing air to billow between fabric and skin.

Ben. Ben. Ben.

I hate that so many things at the LHP remind me of

him now. Life before Ben feels like a dream or some kind of parallel time line. Maybe I *am* living in a bizarre-o version of my life where everything has gone wrong and Ben hasn't been around for months and then I text him and suddenly this letter shows up and he's actually *here*.

I take a seat, and Andrea scooches closer, a ceramic pitcher in her hands. "Miss Stephanie brought some lemonade out while you were showing those kids how to play. Want some?"

My stomach is too shaky. "No thanks."

"You sure? She said to make sure everyone gets a drink."

"I'm fine. I drank some water at the homestead."

"Suit yourself, but, no offense, you don't look so good. Your cheeks are super white."

I sit on my hands, fingernails gripping the rough wooden edge of the porch. "It's not the heat."

Andrea leans in closer, whispering. "Was it that note?"

I nod without looking at her.

"If something's wrong, why don't you talk to your mom? I'll cover for you if Miss Stephanie asks."

It isn't the worst idea. And maybe Mom has seen Ben. She knows everything that happens at the park. Then I don't have to do what this stupid note says. That way I can keep Chloe—

Hold the freaking phone. Chloe's already involved. Her *name* is in the note. Did she just lie to me at the general store? Did she know Ben was coming?

This day is way too complicated, and it's only 10:30.

I stand. "You sure it's cool if I leave?"

"Sure. There's only a little bit of our shift left anyway."

"Thanks, Andrea. I'll see you at the schoolhouse."

"Good luck!"

I'll take all the luck I can get.

9

Saturday, September 11, 2021

Dear Albert,

Ben finally made up his mind.

He'll help me and Chloe with the proposal under one condition: absolutely no research from his house. "My parents would lose their minds if they found out I'm helping with some gay project." (The fact that he's even saying "gay" is kind of a big deal, but this isn't exactly the way I was hoping to hear it. . . .)

It sucks that Ben's parents are so narrow-minded, but I'm not complaining about him having to hang at my house. Chloe, Ben, and I had our first official team research day last weekend; and, Albert, it's still hard to find queer people in American history. After I found you, I figured there had to be more, and I *think* there are, but finding reliable sources is hard.

Last Saturday, Ben figured out that the problem is the words themselves. We were sprawled on the floor in the living room, eating pizza after a long day at the LHP. He was using my phone to research (Ben's paranoid that his parents will find out, even though I told him we can clear the search history on his phone) when, through a mouthful of cheese and pepperoni, he said, "Wait—what?"

"Find something good?" Chloe asked. She was pouring herself another cup of Dr Pepper.

Ben swallowed. "Did you know that the word 'homosexual' didn't even *exist* until 1869? Some guy in Germany invented it."

"I didn't know that," I said. I knew that the word "gay" didn't mean homosexual until the 1950s, but "homosexual" . . . it just seems like an old, science-y word. Albert, I have lots of questions now. Does that mean until the 1950s we didn't have words to describe gay people? That can't be right. (I'm going to bring this up at our next GSA meeting.)

"So for sixty-nine years of the nineteenth century the word 'homosexual' wasn't even a thing?" Chloe slumped to the floor, picked up her phone, and wagged it at us. "How are we supposed to prove any of this if we keep striking out with the only words we *do* have?"

"Lesbian," "gay," "bisexual," "trans," "queer," and now "homosexual"—we thought we'd finally found a word that reached back far enough in history. I shoved Mom's laptop to the side and sat up. "We can prove it. If we can just find the right words, I know we'll find better evidence."

"Um," said Chloe. "*Evidence* is what I'm concerned about."

"You guys." Ben had a funny, far-off look. "If 'homosexual' as, like, an actual *word*, didn't exist until 1869 . . . how is anything about it in the Bible?"

Chloe and I looked at each other. We try to steer clear of church talk around Ben. (For the record, Chloe and I have not gone to a single "new believers night" at Ben's church, and he hasn't been allowed to come to church with us.) Since we believe VERY different things, I didn't see any point in us getting into an argument over what the Bible says, but then he had to go and ask that question.

"There are a lot of things about the Bible that just don't make sense," said Chloe.

I took a slightly more direct approach. "It's in the Bible but it shouldn't be. Pastor Shirt says that over the last hundred years, translators have added 'homosexual' where it doesn't belong."

Ben's face was all wrinkles, like his skin was straining just as hard as his brain to think. "But the Bible is God's Word. How can people just change words?"

Chloe laughed. "Because they're *people*. People do all sorts of things just because they want to. Doesn't make it right."

His face got so scrunched I almost went for Mom's wrinkle cream. As I have previously stated: Ben has a face that is nice. I will do what I must to keep it that way.

"I gotta think about this." Ben bit into another slice of pizza. He chewed slowly, like every bite was a more complicated thought. When Ben finally realized Chloe and I hadn't said anything for a while, he said, "Have you two found anything interesting?"

I wanted to know so badly what he was thinking, Albert. I still do. But I haven't had the courage to bring it back up to him, and he hasn't said a thing about it to me or Chloe.

In my own googling I've found some articles about men who had romantic relationships with each other during the Civil War, but a lot of the articles are from scholarly journals I don't have full access to. But it at least gives me hope—I know we LGBTQ+ people didn't just suddenly spring up out of the ground like daisies in 1869.

There's this author and poet, though, Walt Whitman, who I hadn't heard about until I started researching you. I guess he's pretty famous. Even though words like "gay" and "bisexual" didn't exist when he was alive, it sounds like people knew he was super into dudes and maybe a little into ladies. One of his most famous poems, "O Captain! My Captain!", was written after Abraham Lincoln was assassinated. Here's the last few lines of it:

My Captain does not answer, his lips are pale and still;
My father does not feel my arm, he has no pulse nor will;
The ship is anchor'd safe and sound, its voyage closed and done;

From fearful trip, the victor ship comes in with object won:
Exult, O shores, and ring, O bells!
But I, with mournful tread,
Walk the deck my Captain lies,
Fallen cold and dead.

I wonder if you read this poem. I wonder how you felt when Abraham Lincoln died. You fought for him and you lived in the same state. I wonder if the three of you ever crossed paths—you and Walt Whitman and Abraham Lincoln.

I showed the poem to Ben, since Abraham Lincoln is sort of a thing for us, and he already knew about it! ("Oh, yeah. Mom makes us read a lot of poetry. I like Whitman, but I'm more of a Dickinson fan.")

After we finished eating, we all lay on the floor around Mom's laptop, watching funny YouTube videos. It's not a big screen, so we had to get close to see. I know this has nothing to do with our VERY IMPORTANT RESEARCH, but Ben's leg was millimeters from mine, and I could feel the warmth hovering around him, and then my heart started racing, and while we were laughing at Cat Video number 47, all I could think was:

Is his heart racing, too?
Does he still think I have a nice face?
Move your leg closer, Amos—see what he does.

So, then I did. Just to see. No big deal. I moved real slow, like I was just stretching out my calf muscle, and when my leg came back down my skin slid against his hairyish leg. Weird heat bubbled up from my toes.

The best part? He didn't pull away. Granted, he didn't seem to notice either, but he didn't pull away! I'll take the win.

I wonder what would happen if he was honest with himself, if he could just admit what (I think) he's feeling. Would it really be so bad?

Then again, maybe I'm wrong and he's just a nice guy who isn't afraid to let guys know when they have nice faces?

I don't know.

Today, a week after all that, we had another research day at my house, though it took us a while to get started. Ben brought over a new *Avatar: The Last Airbender*–themed skittles board he's been working on. He and Chloe are both super into the show. The goal of his version is to make it from the South Pole to the North Pole, passing through the Fire Nation and the Earth Kingdom. He even fit in a couple of Air Temples. The top is Aang, the avatar, and you earn points by "finding" (knocking down) skittles painted like Katara and Zuko, but you *lose* points if you run into bad guys like Fire Lord Ozai.

They made me watch a few episodes, and now I'm hooked. It's all super nerdy, but Ben's majorly proud of his craftsmanship, which I'll admit *is* pretty impressive. I've never used a power tool and I wouldn't have thought to build my own skittles board, let alone dream up a whole new set of rules.

Speaking of rules, Chloe's decided to shake things up at the Living History Park even more than we are already.

"I know what I want to do for my apprenticeship," she announced after knocking down five good guys and one bad guy on the *Avatar* board.

The winter of your eighth-grade year you can apply to apprentice in one of the main buildings around the Living History Park instead of traveling from exhibit to exhibit doing random things.

"What?" I asked, resetting the skittles for my turn. I've always wanted to work in the printshop. There's something magical about the smell of the ink, the individual letters sorted into tiny boxes, and the massive printing press that used to spit out daily editions of the *Chickaree County Herald*.

Nowadays, all you really have to do in the printshop is talk about the printing process and ink some fresh leaflets from the handpress. It's low-key, but I love it.

"You know how my parents are always talking about how proud they are of my sister, Cadence? How she's the first person in our family to do *everything*." She started listing on her fingers. "Get a training bra, learn to drive, go to a four-year college, and all that. Well, now it's *my* turn to do something first. Something BIG." Chloe got really serious and took an extralong pause. "I'm going to be the first Black woman blacksmith ever at the LHP."

Ben and I looked at each other. I said, "Um, *can* girls be blacksmiths?"

"You're joking, right?" Chloe's excitement turned into annoyance.

Ben fumbled. "We just—I mean, I've *never* heard of a woman blacksmith."

Chloe shook her head in disbelief, like we'd totally missed something so obvious. "But that's the whole point! Doing all this research on Albert got me thinking about what people supposedly could and couldn't do in the past. A Black girl like me wouldn't have had many options back then, but now I do, and I want to portray a free Black woman blacksmith. I've been doing my own research. It wasn't common, but there totally *were* lady blacksmiths. A whole bunch during the Civil War, when all the men went off to fight."

"Has the LHP ever had a woman blacksmith?" Ben asked as he reset the skittles.

"Or a Black blacksmith?" I added. It felt kind of weird asking that, but I was also glad we were actually *talking* about race.

Chloe shook her head. "Not that I know of, but isn't that what our proposal is all about? Getting the truth out there about all the people the history books forgot to include?

What about *my* truth? What about *my* ancestors? We need to tell as many untold stories as we can."

"You're right," I said, winding up the Aang top. "There are *so* many identities that have been erased or misrepresented. Chloe, this is awesome! How can we help?"

"With research maybe? And backing me up when I talk to your mom about it?" she said. "Not sure what she'll think, since there hasn't been a Black or woman blacksmith at the LHP before."

"I don't think Mom will care if you want to apprentice in the shop," I said, lining up the top in the grooved end of the board and pulling the string fast. The top sped through the South Pole and into the Earth Kingdom, knocking down Sokka, Toph, and Azula (one of the bad guys—not part of the plan). "Actually, she'll probably love the idea!"

"You really think so?" Chloe brightened.

"How could she not?" Ben chimed. "You're awesome."

"Ha, thanks," she said, red warming her light brown cheeks. And I got weirdly jealous because, Albert, what if Ben like-*likes* Chloe's face just as much (*or more*) than mine?

But I shoved my jealousy aside, held out the top-winding string, and said, "Who's up next?"

Chloe took the string from me. "I got this."

I've been thinking about how I can support Chloe even more now. She's been such an incredible friend to me. And not just a friend—an ally. She even joined the Gender and

Sexuality Alliance this year. Not too many straight people do. It meant a lot that Chloe did that for me.

At our GSA meeting this past week, I tried to get some of my other friends excited about the exhibit proposal. We were sitting in the library by the manga, talking about ways we could be more visible in the community. I thought our proposal project was a *perfect* fit.

"I don't know, Amos," said Azul, our club president. They're short, Latinx, and have more energy than a toddler. Their hair has been dyed sapphire blue as long as I've known them. "No offense, but history is kinda boring."

Kevin looked up from the manga she was reading. She has short, reddish-brown hair and pale almost translucent skin. She was wearing her favorite Naruto shirt. "Unless we're talking about medieval times. Then I'm all in." Kevin's first name is Daphne, but she goes by her old Irish middle name, which has been passed down through her family for generations. She's bi and has a super dry sense of humor. "I've always wanted a sword."

"No swords, Kevin," I said.

"Unless I make one," Chloe added, wiggling her eyebrows. I shook my head at her quickly.

"*I* think we should have a bake sale." If a birch tree came to life, that would be Cassidy. She's tall, pale, kind of flaky. Hips tilted in a semipermanent lean. She goes by she/they and she's only ever said she's interested in girls.

Cassidy went on: "We could donate the money we make to the Trevor Project!"

Obviously, you don't know what the Trevor Project is, Albert. It's this incredible organization that supports LGBTQ+ kids. You can call or text and talk to someone any time of the day.

"OMG," said Azul. "Yes! We can bake *rainbow sugar cookies*."

And then I lost them. Cassidy, Azul, and Kevin can be kind of cliquey. We all call them the Gay Cerberus. They aren't *actually* a rainbow-spewing mythical three-headed dog beast from Hades, but they're never apart. It's freaky. Also, they gave themselves that nickname. I don't think nicknames really work that way, but WHATEVER.

And once the Gay Cerberus agrees on something, it's IMPOSSIBLE to get them to change their minds. Cassidy's idea was a good one, so I didn't really mind. Raising money for the Trevor Project is super important. I know kids in our group have called them before when they've gotten super low. I guess the proposal project can just stay me, Chloe, and Ben. I wish Ben could come to a GSA meeting. I think he'd like the other kids.

UGH. I wish a lot of things for Ben. And I wish I didn't have to.

Your friend,

Amos Abernathy

10

★ ★ ★

New Hope Church
Saturday, August 13, 2022—10:41 a.m.

"Ma, do you mind if I speak with you for a moment?"

She's chatting with one of the craft vendors who's selling quilting squares. She holds up a finger to me. Sounds like they're negotiating something about vendor fees for next year.

"I'll be quick," I say.

Mom sighs. "I'm so sorry. I'll be right back, Marge." Mom and I walk off toward the church, and she says, "What's going on, Amos?"

And there it is again. That tone, like she's asking a question she already knows the answer to. Maybe this was a bad idea.

But if Ben's here, I need to know. "You haven't seen Ben around today, have you?" I ask.

Mom frowns—guess she wasn't expecting that question. Then her face squinches like she's ticking through all the

Bens she knows until she says, "Wait, Ben? *Ben*-Ben?" Her voice lowers. "Ben Oglevie?"

"Yes, that Ben."

"I thought you two weren't speaking anymore. Did I miss something?"

"No, and we're not," I say, peering over her shoulder, like just saying his name might make him appear.

Mom follows my gaze behind her. "What's going on? If something's happened again—"

"Nothing's happened. I'm fine."

I avoid her eyes as she studies me. "Your face says otherwise."

"I shouldn't have said anything. If you haven't seen him, it's not a big deal." I turn to leave, even more frustrated than before.

She grabs my arm. "Amos, wait." I don't pull away, but I don't turn around either. I've got to find Ben. "Come here," she says, and leads me, reluctantly, to the steps of New Hope Church.

"I'm fine, Mom," I say, slumping next to her on the steps. "Forget I said anything about Ben."

In her hand appears a white handkerchief with pink chrysanthemums embroidered in the corner. She dabs my forehead, smoothing aside my hair. "Have you been drinking enough water?"

"Yes. Can I go now? I need to get to the schoolhouse."

Oof. That sounded way harsher than I meant. I add quickly, "I know you're busy."

The handkerchief retracts, folds in half, then in quarters, then eighths, until it disappears between her clenched palms. A heavy wind rolls over us. Fresh sweat runs down my face. The chatter of the LHP dims, but only for us.

This is the kind of silence I've learned to wait on, the sort of quiet that hovers before someone yells "Charge!" I brace myself.

"It's all right if you miss Ben," she says, and I'm officially confused. Mom goes on: "Things may have ended badly between you two, but just because something ends, it doesn't mean it's over. Not for everyone involved, at least."

I don't want to admit that she's right. "It's fine. I'm over him."

"Well, if you weren't, that would be okay, too." She pauses. "Why did you ask me if I'd seen him today?"

I swat a fly buzzing around my nose. "It's nothing."

"Amos, don't make me drag it out of you. I know when something's up."

Ugh. Coming to see Mom was a trap. "I got a note."

"A note? What kind of note? From Ben?"

"Yes."

"Did he give it to you? What did he say? Are you okay? I—"

"Whoa, Nelly." I half laugh, shaking my head. "He left

the note for me at the Wakefield House. I haven't seen him yet."

She grunts. "Sounds like Ben."

For some reason, that comment heats me up. "It's not his fault."

"You're right," she says. "I'm sorry. It's not *all* his fault. I just . . . I just want to protect you. So, what does the note say?"

"He wants to talk."

The handkerchief reappears, unfolding itself. "Do *you* want to talk?"

"Ugh, I don't know." I fidget with the strap of my haversack. "I'm glad he wants to talk, but I feel like *I'm* the one that should get to do the talking. He shouldn't get the first word when he already had the last."

"I see." The handkerchief falls to Mom's lap. She holds my knee. "That's a lot for you to think about today, with everything else going on. You've got a lot on your plate this afternoon."

Hot as it is, my breath goes subzero in my chest. *She knows, she knows, she knows, she knows.* I'm afraid if I look at her, she'll see the fear in my eyes. If Mom ruins our plan, I swear I won't be able to handle it. Not that *and* Ben turning up.

"What?" she says. "You didn't forget about the battle, did you?"

My lungs unfreeze. "Oh, ha ha, no, right. Totally. The battle—yeah, that's got me a little overwhelmed."

She doesn't know, she doesn't know, she doesn't know.

"Does the note say when Ben wants to talk? Maybe all this can wait until after the battle reenactment?"

"It just says to let Chloe know if I'm 'willing' to talk."

Her eyebrows rise. "Chloe? How's she involved in all this?"

My eyebrows bunch together. "I—I'm not sure. But whatever's going on, I know Chloe's got my back."

But I'm wondering if that's true now. Has she been keeping something from me?

But Mom says, "You're right. Why don't you start by talking to Chloe, and I'll keep an eye out for Ben? If I spot him, I'll come find you."

"Yeah. Okay." I nod. But then I imagine her going all Mama Bear on him and I say, "But if you do, please don't say anything to him. This is between me and him."

Her hands fly up in mock surrender. "Lord knows I've already put in my two cents."

"More like a million cents—"

"There you are, hon." Darren appears, already suited up in his Union blues even though the battle isn't for a while yet. "I've been looking all over for you."

Mom's whole face lights up. "Hey, sweetie. What's going on?"

Hon.

Sweetie.

Barf.

"And that's my cue," I say. "Mom, I'll be at the schoolhouse if, uh, anything comes up, okay? Later, Darren."

Mom nods meaningfully. "Sounds good."

"See you at the battle, Amos! Don't forget we're meeting at noon to practice a bit beforehand," Darren hollers, his wide hand waving at me.

I wave back, heading off to meet Chloe at the schoolhouse for our next shift, when I hear someone call my name. "AaaaaaaaaaaMOOOOOOOS!"

Uh-oh.

11

Friday, September 17, 2021

Dear Albert,

Shoes.

Shoes.

That's Meredith Simmons's great idea for the exhibit proposal to replace the "Heroes of the Nineteenth Century." She's been running around talking up her plans: urban versus rural shoes, the "heeling" power of fashion, the worker's "sole." She's calling the project "A Step into the Past: Nineteenth-Century Footwear and You."

I just . . . I can't.

To make it worse, everyone at the LHP actually seems excited about the idea. Mom and I were standing outside the printshop, talking with Mrs. Weaver, the shop's cranky lead interpreter, when Meredith came by with a fat stack of sunshine-yellow paper and a smug grin. Mindy waved meekly behind her.

"You put this together yourself?" Mom asked, scanning the sheet.

"We did, Miss Abernathy," Meredith said. "Mindy and I. Daddy thought it would be a good idea to get other people excited about our proposal. Community support is so important when it comes to change."

Albert, I don't think my eyes could have rolled back far enough. *Community support is so important when it comes to change?* Really? I've never heard Meredith string words together like that. It sounded way more like her dad talking, which doesn't surprise me. Like I said, the Simmons dynasty has ruled over Chickaree County for decades. Her parents own half of downtown Apple Grove, including an organic grocery and, if you were paying attention, their *shoe* store.

"A little advertising doesn't hurt either," Mrs. Weaver said, snagging a second flyer with her wrinkly white hand. "A thirty percent off coupon is a generous discount at Shoe In."

"Daddy wants everyone to know how invested he is in the LHP," Meredith said. "He said it was the least he could do."

Gag me.

"I'll admit I'm impressed," said Mom. (This is the moment I almost disowned her.)

"Looks like you've really put some thought into this." Mrs. Weaver folded the flyers into her apron. "Can't imagine many people have gotten this far on their proposals yet."

I wanted to jump in about our project, but I didn't have anything to show. And I wasn't sure how Mrs. Weaver would react to something about LGBTQ+ history. She's a Holy Crosser, too. More times than I can count, I've heard her start her tour with: "It was a simpler time. No emails, no texting, no video chats. For the most part, if folks wanted the news, they had no other choice than the local newspaper." But we all know it wouldn't have been easier for people like you and me, Albert. Not for Chloe. Not for Ben either. (Maybe.)

Let's be real. It still isn't. Which is exactly why we're doing this. People, especially like Mrs. Weaver, who teach others what the past was like, need to know that people like us have *always* existed.

Okay, end rant. (For now.)

"You know there isn't going to be a countywide vote or anything, right?" Mom said to Meredith. "It's up to me and the board to decide on the new exhibit."

Meredith twisted her hair between her thumb and pointer finger. "Doesn't hurt to get everyone excited. And, you know what Daddy said? He said he'd be willing to contribute even *more* to the Living History Park if a great idea like this goes through. Something that really connects the past to the present. An exhibit that really engages the community."

I tried to give Mom a covert look of disgust, but it must

not have been so covert because she shot me a look right back that said "Cut it out."

Here's the awful thing, Albert: Mom seems legitimately impressed with Meredith and Mindy's idea. She praised their "initiative," as if Ben, Chloe, and I haven't taken all the initiative in the world.

There's no way I'm letting shoes be more important than queer people.

That's when I knew we had to level up our proposal strategy for Forgotten Voices. So, Chloe and I decided to go to the coolest history buff we know, our social studies teacher Ms. Wiseman. She's pretty much the living embodiment of Wikipedia. She's young, white, probably not even thirty. Patterned jumpers are her favorite thing, and she almost always has her black, curly hair wrapped in a bandanna. She's even got a nose ring. In other words, she's the most awesome adult we know.

So, today, Chloe and I stayed behind after the bell rang. "Hey, Ms. W," I said while she rewrote the opening question for the next class on the whiteboard. "I was wondering if you could help me and Chloe with something?"

"I charge extra between classes."

Yeah, she tries to be funny like that.

"Don't worry—we tip well." Chloe's just as quick.

Ms. Wiseman lowered the dry-erase marker. "Shoot."

After a deep breath, I told her about the LHP taking

exhibit proposals and our idea to showcase LGBTQ+ stories from the nineteenth century, especially stories close to home. Ms. Wiseman started chewing on the end of her dry-erase marker, nodding while I spoke. She only chews on pens and things when she's thinking something through, so I took that as a good sign.

"Well, Meredith Simmons, you know her—squeaky voice, thinks she's better than everyone, kind of a bigot, family could buy a small isla—"

"I know who she is, Amos."

"Right, so, Meredith Simmons and Mindy Liu have this proposal idea about, get this, *shoes*, and they already have flyers and are, like, *campaigning* for their idea, even though it's not *actually* a competition or an election or anything. My point is, I want the new exhibit to be something that really matters."

Ms. Wiseman dropped the dry-erase marker into the whiteboard tray. "Okay."

"Okay, so—" I breathed in, struggling to believe that I really had to put this together for her (I mean, Ms. Wiseman has a *master's degree* . . .). "Meredith Simmons might have all the money in the world, and her parents might run half the town, but what they don't have is an expert backing them up."

And there it was. The twin light bulbs winked on in Ms. Wiseman's almost black eyes. Her lips curled into something between a smile and a smirk. "I see."

Here's the thing about Ms. Wiseman that I haven't mentioned yet: aside from being the best teacher at Apple Grove Middle School and a brilliant, highly educated history teacher with a master's degree in American history from the University of Chicago, she's also the school sponsor for our Gender and Sexuality Alliance.

Albert, she's one of us. She even keeps a picture of her girlfriend next to her desktop computer. Ms. Wiseman is the only out and proud teacher I've ever had, and it probably takes a lot of courage for her to be, especially in Chickaree County, where there aren't so many of us. She said she and her girlfriend sometimes get weird looks when they go out to eat.

"So, will you help us?" Chloe asked.

Ms. Wiseman took a deep breath, checking the clock as a bunch of kids rushed into the room, laughing and yelling. "Let me think on it," she said. "Send me an email with what you've got so far, and we can chat tomorrow after school, if that's okay with your parents."

Just like that, I knew we had her, and the chances of our proposal getting picked doubled. No—TRIPLED. What now, Meredith Simmons!

Chloe came home with me this afternoon. We called Ben over so we could tell him the good news. Together we put everything we have in an email—you, Walt Whitman, the free Black women from Connecticut, a bunch about women soldiers who dressed as men to fight, and some scandalous romantic stuff about a few sailors during the war—and shot it off to her.

I don't know why we expected a response right away, but we refreshed my inbox for a good half hour before we gave up and played Mario Party instead.

It's almost nine and I just checked again—still nothing.

I'm having trouble falling asleep. With Ms. Wiseman's help, we'd really have a chance. If she says no, I don't know how we're going to one-up Meredith and Mindy.

Your friend,

Amos Abernathy

12

New Hope Church
Saturday, August 13, 2022—10:53 a.m.

"AMOS!"

No, no, no, no, *no*—the Gay Cerberus. Not here. Not now!

I bolt down the steps of the church.

"Guys, what are you doing here?" I try to pull them behind a vendor's tent and out of Mom's sight as much as possible. "I told you to get here around one and to head straight to the main stage."

Azul wriggles out of my grasp. Their blue hair flaps around their shoulders as they bounce around me. "What's the big deal? We got excited, so we came early. OMG—we cannot *wait* for this afternoon. Are you nervous? Is that why you're acting weird? Because you're acting weird."

"Yeah, yeah. Just, come over here. And not so loud." I make the mistake of looking over my shoulder, and

Mom's staring right at us, even though she's still talking to Darren.

"You sure you're okay, Amos?" says Cassidy, the long braid down her back swinging as she looks at me.

I step in front of her gaze, which had followed mine to Mom.

"I'm fine," I say. This is what I get for lying to too many people. Mom doesn't know what's coming this afternoon . . . but I had to tell the Gay Cerberus, the other GSA kids, and Ms. Wiseman that Mom was in full support of our performance. They wouldn't have agreed to do it otherwise. I try to cover up my worry with a big smile. "I just wasn't expecting you yet and the timing of all of this is super important so—"

Kevin, who's been staring at my armpits this whole time, interrupts. "You sweat a lot."

I cross my arms. "Uh, thanks?"

Kevin nods. "You're welcome."

"Can we, like, drop off our stuff for later somewhere?" asks Cassidy. A bulging backpack is bending her to the ground even more than usual.

Familiar footsteps approach. "Who're your friends, Amos?"

I knew it. Mom just couldn't stay away. But I can do this. Keep everyone in the dark until the last possible second.

103

I turn to her, and through a grin I say, "Just some friends from school."

Azul's hand springs from their body. "Hi, Ms. Abernathy. I'm Azul Rodriguez, president of the GSA at Apple Grove Middle School. I just wanted to say thank you for letting us—"

Oh my god, oh my god, OH MY GOD.

I blurt. "For letting you experience another great Civil War Remembrance Week celebration, right?" Now I'm really sweating.

Azul's head leans to the left, oblivious to my *do-not-speak* glare. "I mean, yeah, that, too, I guess, but I meant—"

"Oh boy!" I say, ushering the Gay Cerberus away from Mom. "We're gonna be late for my next shift at the schoolhouse and you all *promised to go with me.*"

"Amos, what are y—"

I don't give Azul time to question me. "See you later, Mom."

I hook Cassidy's and Kevin's arms in mine.

Cassidy's free arm sways in the breeze. "See you later, Ms. Abernathy!"

"I like your shoes, Ms. A.," Kevin says. "Bye!"

"Uh, thanks," Mom says. "You kids enjoy yourselves. And don't be late, Amos!"

"I won't!"

I hold on tight until Mom's out of sight.

"What was all that about?" asks Azul. "I wanted to thank your mom for letting us do our thing this afternoon."

"You can thank her afterward," I say.

Kevin's eyes narrow on my nose. "You're not telling us something. You always sniff a lot when you're lying."

"No, I don't," I say. "I just—no talking to my mom, okay?"

Cassidy hikes the backpack higher up on her shoulder. "Your mom's nice. Why can't we talk to her?"

"Are we embarrassing you?" Azul scoffs. "So much for—"

Getting more frustrated by the second, I cut them off. "No, it's not that. I just need you to listen to me."

"Oh, I get it now." Kevin nods pensively. "Your mom doesn't know."

Ughhhhhh. Kevin. Stop being so smart.

Azul hops in place. "Doesn't know what?"

My lips don't budge, but Kevin goes on. "About this afternoon. Our performance."

Azul's and Cassidy's eyes bug out of their heads. *"What?"*

Crap. They're totally going to bail. *Think, Amos!*

"It's fine!" I blurt. "It's just—it's supposed to be a—a . . . surprise."

The Gay Cerberus speaks as one. "A *surprise?*"

They're so not buying this, but I can't go back now. "Yeah. A surprise. So, don't say anything! To anyone." I

105

point to the right, across the park. "Now head over to the main stage. There's a white tent in back. You can put your stuff there. I've got to go."

I really do. My next shift starts at the schoolhouse in less than a minute. I wave goodbye and book it. My haversack slaps against my thigh.

This day is getting way too complicated.

13

Thursday, October 7, 2021

Dear Albert,

I had to wait until the next morning for the email, but Ms. Wiseman finally said YES! We got together that afternoon, then this past Tuesday, and now today we met for the third time to go over our notes. I've done research papers for English and one for Ms. Wiseman, but those papers were on topics most people know about. Researching LGBTQ+ history is like being a paleontologist on the hunt for a complete dinosaur skeleton and, after days of chipping away, only finding a molar.

"Language is constantly evolving," Ms. Wiseman told us while we were sitting at a row of computers in the media center. "It's likely our understanding of sexuality and gender—identity as a whole—will shift again in the next ten, twenty, thirty years. The thing is, we don't know what we don't know. That makes looking back in history a challenge. Ultimately, we won't be able to decide if someone would have identified as 'gay' or 'lesbian' or 'trans'—I wouldn't want someone assuming my identity if I wasn't explicit about it, either—*but* we can look for evidence in the way individuals lived to support the idea that they *could* have identified as a member of the LGBTQ+ community."

Sometimes with Ms. Wiseman, it's like being in a high school or college level class. And she's getting way more into this than I would have expected. She'll go on about certain things Chloe and I don't know about, but we're trying to keep up. Honestly, Ms. Wiseman is kind of becoming my new queero.

Well, after you, of course.

The thing about the internet, Albert, is that the *basic* internet doesn't give you many reliable sources. For things everyone should know, like "where was pizza invented" or "why is the sky blue," you can use all sorts of websites, but doing *this* research is way harder. Ms. Wiseman keeps reminding us that we need to pay attention to the types of sources we're using: primary (actual artifacts from the era, like journals, newspapers, and letters), secondary (text-books, articles about primary sources, etc.), or tertiary (an index or bibliography). What we really need is access to these giant digital warehouses full of primary documents, like Walt Whitman's letters and Civil War soldiers' diaries and actual newspaper clippings from 1861.

Guess who's got the hookup? Ms. Wiseman! She can

still get into all the library services her graduate program gave her, so we've been able to take our research and our credibility up a notch. We finally have the exact proof we've been missing, *and* a teacher backing us up. This is HUGE.

"Hey, take a look at this," Chloe said, calling us over to her screen.

She pointed to a transcription of a journal from a Civil War seaman who'd been stationed along the Virginia coast. Ms. Wiseman and I read it over her shoulder. My cheeks got all hot and I felt kind of weird reading the letter with Ms. Wiseman there—it's not that the letter was inappropriate, but this white man CLEARLY had a thing for another dude. You can tell by the way he describes him . . . and the fact that they shared a bunk.

Side note: I guess it was super common for people of the same gender to share a bed during the nineteenth century. Tiny rooms, little space, not enough heat. That makes it harder to know when people were in bed together because they had to be or because they *wanted* to be.

Albert, I wasn't expecting to think this much about beds when I started this project. When it comes to evidence like this, I try to act cool about it because that's what Ms. Wiseman does. All she said when she read the letter was, "That's solid. Print off a copy and we'll add it to the binder."

That's right, Albert. We're a month away from the proposal due date, and we already have a BINDER of documents with color-coded tabs and multicolor dividers. In fact, we have enough evidence in place that I decided we're ready to make our proposal public—if Meredith and Mindy are getting everyone hyped, so can we.

Every Sunday, Pastor Shirt sets time aside at the end of his sermon for the congregation to ask for prayer requests or share something going on in their lives. I've never spoken until this past weekend.

You should have seen Mom's face when I stood up. She was surprised, like my legs had been broken all my life and started working suddenly.

"Amos Abernathy!" Pastor Shirt said. He's got a superhero jawline, golden white skin, and a thing for Hawaiian shirts. "What a nice surprise. How can we be present for you today?"

Everyone was watching me, but no one more intently than Mom. I cleared my throat. "My friends Ben Oglevie, Chloe Thompson, and I are working on a proposal for a new LHP exhibit that tells the stories of LGBTQ+ people who lived in the nineteenth century. Our goal is to prove that queer people have a place in history, including Illinois's very own Albert D. J. Cashier, someone who we might consider a transgender man today, who fought for the Union during the Civil War and lived out the rest of his days in Saunemin. So, I guess I was wondering if everyone could keep our work in your prayers, and if you have any questions, let me know!"

I sat back down so quickly the seat squeaked. Mom squeezed my knee, which meant she wasn't mad. That was a relief.

Pastor Shirt's trademark, full-face smile glowed in my direction. "Sounds like you're doing a work of love, Amos. A work of true love. It'll be a joy to keep you all in our prayers."

I felt pretty amazing then, Albert. Pretty freaking amazing.

That didn't last long.

Later, while Mom was chatting with her Bible study ladies, Jessica and her girlfriend, Trish, found me waiting outside the sanctuary. "Hey, Amos!"

"We just wanted to let you know how awesome you are," Trish said. She's Black and has rich, dark brown skin. She was wearing killer heels and a tangerine blazer. "If there's any way we can help out with your proposal, beyond praying of course, let us know. Queers unite!"

"Thanks." I laughed. "I will."

Jessica leaned in, tucking her tawny hair behind her pink ear. "Did you say an *Oglevie* was helping you out?"

The way she said that made my stomach drop. "Yeah, Ben."

"That's . . . unexpected," she said.

I wanted to cry. I'd been so caught up in my nerves that

I forgot Ben probably wouldn't want his name attached to our VERY GAY proposal. I hadn't exactly *outed* him, but I had betrayed him. *Big*-time. How could I be so stupid? Of *course*, Jessica knew the Oglevies from going to Holy Cross. And if she knew them, who else did? I stared at the water stain on my shoe.

"And his parents are cool with that?" she asked.

Lying in church isn't something I do, but this time I couldn't help it. "Not sure what he's told them." (Except I am sure: he's told them absolutely nothing.)

Jessica nodded thoughtfully, pulling down the sleeves of her sweater. "Well, just keep an eye out for him. My parents and the Oglevies, they're not that different. If you know what I mean."

"I think I do."

She hesitated before adding, "And maybe, uh, maybe don't mention him next time you talk about the project?"

My face burned up, but I said, "Yeah, I can do that."

I've felt off ever since that conversation. Guilty. We might live in the same town, but Ben and I are from different worlds. It makes me sick thinking what happened to Jessica could happen to him, even if he's not actually, you know, gay. Even if he's just helping Chloe and me out because he's a good friend. I have no idea what his parents might do.

You have no idea how much I wish Ben didn't go to

Holy Cross. How much I wish he wasn't homeschooled. I actually asked him about that this week.

"Have you ever thought about going to public school?"

We were sitting in my living room. Chloe had just left, and Ben's brother was on his way to pick him up. (It was only like 7:30, but Mom has rules about how late I can have friends over on a school night.)

He closed our research binder and looked at me. "I've *thought* about it, but I don't know."

My heart crammed a little tighter into my ribs. He's thought about it, Albert, and the way he said "thought," I mean, it kind of felt like he was implying that I was part of his thinking. But maybe I imagined that. "What do you mean you don't know?"

He pushed his hair off his forehead. "All my brothers were—or still are—being homeschooled through high school. Mom was homeschooled all the way through, too. It's like this unspoken family tradition. It's all I've ever known, and, I know this sounds weird to most people, but I actually *like* being homeschooled."

I laughed. "Who wouldn't like sleeping in every day?"

He smiled but shook his head. "That's nice, don't get me wrong, but we work a lot. If I sleep in, I still have all my subjects to get through during the day. I just get to do most of my work when I want to do it. And if I want to research something in depth or explore a new idea, I can."

"Not every new idea," I didn't say.

"I guess that would be kind of awesome," I said. "Sometimes I wish we could move faster through classes, especially math. It's like, I *get it*, but then not everyone does, and we can't move on until the whole class is on the same page."

Ben nodded. "Right. At home, I'm the only one on the page. If I get it, we're on to the next thing. Simple as that."

I sank down off the couch and onto the floor, closer to him. "What about friends, though?" I asked. "Don't you wish you could see more people?"

"I see people," he said defensively. "Our homeschool group, you and Chloe, the other LHP kids."

"But we could hang out all the time, have classes together, eat lunch together."

He nodded. "Yeah, I know. Honestly, I didn't care so much when I was little, not with all my brothers around. We had each other and our neighbors, and I've got lots of cousins. It all felt like enough." He scratched his nose. "I haven't told anyone this, but last year, this weird loneliness set in. Even with everyone at home, it was like I was in this bubble, still there but . . . separate from everyone else. That's one of the reasons I started volunteering at the LHP."

I pulled my knees up to my chest. "I thought your mom made you volunteer. For a school project?"

"That sounded a little better than 'I didn't have anyone

114

to talk to.'" His cheeks reddened and he looked down. "I just—for the first time I felt like I needed someone outside my family."

"Believe me, I get that," I said, leaning in closer so I could lower my voice. Mom was in the kitchen, but she's a total eavesdropper. "I love my mom, but I can't imagine only ever having her to talk to."

That got a small laugh. "You're lucky you have her. She loves you, no matter what."

My heart broke a little. Because what I heard him really say was "I'm not sure my parents will love me no matter what."

I nudged his foot with mine. (It wasn't gross or anything, I was wearing socks.) "Chloe and I, we're here for you no matter what. My mom, too."

Albert, I've mentioned Ben's eyes before. How they're all these different shades of brown. Well, I've noticed that different sorts of emotions bring out different colors. When he's happy, there's this gold glint that sparks, and when he's angry his whole eye turns into this shadowy mudslide. But when he's sad, it's like a kaleidoscope of bronze and copper and the pebbles we find lining Chickaree Lake.

A car horn honked. Ben's brother. I couldn't tell if Ben looked more relieved or frustrated that our conversation got interrupted. He hopped up in a hurry and I followed him to the front door.

"Bye, Ben!" Mom hollered from the kitchen.

"Night, Ms. Abernathy," he called. It was like there was this happy mask hanging over his voice, hiding all the sad.

I couldn't take it. Before he opened the front door, I wrapped my arms around him and just held tight. It was a second before his hands were on my back, fingers hesitant on my shoulder blades, but then we just stayed like that for what felt like forever, my chin on his shoulder, his cheek on mine.

Honk! We pulled apart fast.

His eyes were a little more honey colored than before. "Talk tomorrow?"

I nodded. "Yeah, tomorrow. Good night, Ben."

"Night, Amos."

Having feelings for someone who doesn't like you back is the worst. Even if Ben *is* gay, maybe he's just not into me. Maybe I need to lay off hinting at things and accept that we're just friends and that's all we'll ever be.

This sucks.

Thanks for listening, Albert. (Not that I'm giving you much of a choice. Hope you don't mind.)

Your friend,

Amos Abernathy

14

Logan Schoolhouse
Saturday, August 13, 2022—11:01 a.m.

Our schoolmarm's bell clangs as I run up the gravel path to the little white schoolhouse. I'm pitting out big-time now (*ew*). But the building sits at the top of a clover-clotted hill on the southwest corner of the park, so running was my only option. A small horseshoe of modern-clothed guests has formed around our teacher, Ms. Wiseman. She's one of the few people I know who can wear a calico dress like it's back in style.

"Ah, the last of my young flock," she says loudly, the bell coming to rest at her side. "You were very nearly tardy, Mr. Abernathy."

The cool edge in her voice could be an act, but her arched eyebrow tells me she's actually wondering what's up.

"Sorry, Miss Wiseman." I catch my breath, hands on my knees, playing it up. Guests love the extra drama. "Ma needed help with the chickens. Won't happen again."

"I'm sure it will not." Ms. Wiseman grins, seemingly reassured. "Hurry along inside now."

Ms. Wiseman started volunteering at the LHP this past June when actual school let out. There isn't another teacher I can think of who'd give up any of their summer to spend *more* time thinking about school (and not get paid for it).

She's never said it out loud, but I think she volunteered for me, after how everything went down this past winter. Every time she looks at me, I feel something like pity or guilt, like maybe she thinks she could have done more.

I don't want her pity. And she has nothing to feel guilty about.

I squeeze through the doorway, past the coat hooks and benches, and around the black stove that heats the building in the fall and winter months. Chloe's at a desk in the front, far-left corner of the room. I drop into a wooden desk as close to her as I can get.

Ben's note plays over in my mind. I wish he'd just come talk to me instead of making me go through Chloe. Why is everything so complicated with him? Now I have to waste time checking in with Chloe instead of getting it over with and on with my life!

Unfortunately for me, Meredith Simmons and Mindy Liu are sitting in the desks directly between me and Chloe.

Meredith turns at the wrong time and gets caught in the crossfire of the death stare meant to get Chloe's attention. "What's your problem? My beauty finally turn you straight?" She snickers.

"You wish." (She *does* have a thing for Timothée Chalamet. I'm not saying he and I are twins or anything, but I could pass for him on Halloween.)

"Ha, as if I'd ever—"

I cough, cutting Meredith off. Chloe finally looks at me, but I can't read her expression.

Before I can say anything, Ms. Wiseman leads the visitors in: a pale older Asian couple and two white families with little kids. They fill the space around the desks, sitting on benches along the walls and cramming around the unlit stove. A few of the youngest visitors sit in the empty desks, eyes wide with wonder, like they've never seen a classroom before.

"Welcome, everyone, to the Logan Schoolhouse, originally built in 1812 and used until 1897," Ms. Wiseman declares. "Before we begin our daily lesson, I want to share a little about our school's history." Her arms open wide, palms upward. "As you can see, we don't have much space for our students. In the one-room schoolhouse, children as young as five and as old as thirteen squeezed into tightly packed desks, one teacher instructing them all at the same time." She looks to the visiting children. "Tell me, what do you notice about this school that is different from your present-day schools?"

A small child with long, dark hair raises her hand. "There's no lights."

"That is mostly correct," Ms. Wiseman says. "Lessons were taught almost entirely by natural light, which is why there are so many windows, except on this back wall with the blackboard." She points to two glass globes behind her. "These are gas lamps. They are lit late at night and only if absolutely necessary. What else do you notice?"

My knee bounces. I need to know what Chloe knows about Ben. But she won't look at me now, playing the good student for Ms. Wiseman. I consider tearing a page out of my journal and passing a note, but it would have to get past Meredith and Mindy, so that's a no go.

A boy, a little older, raises his hand. "I don't see any paper or pens. What did you write with?"

Ms. Wiseman looks pleased. "Good eye, young man. Students, please take out your slates and pens." The other LHP kids and I pull our small, rectangular blackboards and thin chalk pens from our haversacks and baskets. Visitors lean in to marvel at the ancient technology. I can't help but crack a smile at the way folks are amazed by such simple things. Ms. Wiseman goes on: "Paper and ink were costly, so students used slates and chalk to write assignments and practice their work. Okay, let's have one more." She calls on a small girl in the third row wearing glasses.

While Ms. Wiseman is busy, I scratch a message on my slate. *Need to talk.*

"Where's the bathroom?" the little girl asks.

I casually prop the slate up in Chloe's direction while Meredith and Mindy pretend to be studious little darlings.

"You might just have the sharpest eyes of all," Ms. Wiseman beams. "The one-room schoolhouse is just that. For the majority of the nineteenth century, indoor plumbing . . ."

Chloe isn't looking. I cough, but only Mindy turns. I flip the chalk message down. She eyes me suspiciously.

"So, we have two outhouses behind the school, one for gentlemen and one for ladies." Ms. Wiseman's hand rises to her cheek like she's letting them in on a secret. "But I recommend doing your business elsewhere."

This gets a small chuckle from the crowd. While they laugh, I take the opportunity to tilt the board up again. I cough, a little louder. This time, Chloe looks back. "Not now," she mouths.

"When?" I mouth back, but she ignores me.

Ugh. I erase the message with my elbow.

"Now, class," Ms. Wiseman continues, "let's begin today's lesson. Please stand and recite the Pledge of Allegiance with me."

121

I turn down my slate and rise with the rest of the class, all of us lifting hands to hearts as we turn toward the flag stationed in the far-right corner. This part of the reenactment always feels strange—I mean, we still say the Pledge in real life, but when the principal at Apple Grove Middle School recites it over the PA system, most kids just stand around awkwardly. Only a few people, mostly teachers, put their hands on their hearts, and almost nobody says the words out loud. I don't get how we went from this to that.

We drone in unison, a few of the visitors chiming in as well, but they fumble over the phrasing. "I pledge allegiance to my flag and the republic for which it stands, one nation, indivisible, with liberty and justice for all."

Ms. Wiseman steps out of character while the other kids and I sit back down. "You'll notice that the words are different from what you might expect. When Francis Bellamy, the author of the original Pledge of Allegiance, published it in 1892, he wanted his words to be spoken by any person in any country, not just America. It wasn't until 1923 that it became specific to American culture, and not until 1954 that we added the phrase 'under God'."

She returns to the blackboard, where she points at the classroom rules written in crisp cursive, the first being "obey thy elders" and the second "speak only when spoken to." While her back is turned, I flip my miniature chalkboard back up with a new message. *Did you know???*

Chloe shakes her head.

Meredith Simmons's hand shoots into the air. "Ms. Wiseman!"

Chloe and I sit bolt upright in our desks.

"Yes, Miss Simmons?"

"Amos and Chloe are sharing secret messages again."

"Is this true, Mr. Abernathy? Miss Thompson?"

Meredith grins wickedly. Chloe and I don't say a word. Ms. Wiseman doesn't know this isn't an act—we aren't playing naughty school children for the visitors!

But getting caught always comes with a punishment. Ms. Wiseman bustles from the blackboard to my desk in three brisk steps. "Stand, Mr. Abernathy. Show me your slate."

I try to tell her what's really going on with my eyes, but Ms. Wiseman isn't picking up what I'm putting down. So, I get up and place the chalk-smudged rectangle in her hand.

She reads it aloud to the class. "'Did you know?' Mr. Abernathy, what precisely were you hoping Miss Thompson would reveal that I could not during our lessons today?"

"Nothing, Miss Wiseman. It's nothing."

"Nothing? I see." Ms. Wiseman swoops back around her desk and pulls open a drawer. "Mr. Abernathy, I do not appreciate you interrupting my class for 'nothing.' Come here."

Cue internal groaning.

Everyone watches me walk forward. The floor creaks. Ms. Wiseman hangs a wooden sign strung with a rope around my neck. "Idle Boy," it reads. She marches me by the shoulders to the right corner of the room next to the American flag. "You'll face this corner for the remainder of class, young man. I hope *this* lesson sinks in."

I glare into the shadows. This is so annoying, but it isn't Ms. Wiseman's fault. Just one more reason to loathe Meredith Simmons.

15

Sunday, October 31, 2021

Dear Albert,

I have MAJOR updates on Ben FREAKING Oglevie, but FIRST I have to tell you about Chloe. SHE TURNED IN HER APPRENTICESHIP APPLICATION. AHHHH!

"Blacksmith, huh?" Mom didn't look up as she scanned Chloe's application. "We've never had a woman blacksmith before. You know it was a male-dominated profession. Few women would have had the physical strength for such a strenuous job, not to mention the fact that they were expected to work in the home."

I coughed. *"Patriarchy!"*

Mom was only mildly amused.

"Far as I know, we haven't had a *Black* blacksmith either," Chloe said. "I want to reenact as a free Black girl mastering a trade, owning her destiny."

Mom's head bobbed slowly. "That would be a powerful message, but . . ."

I didn't like where that "but" was going, so I jumped in. "We've done our research, Mom. Some women totally were blacksmiths. And there were free African Americans living in Illinois . . . eventually."

I realized that maybe I'd said too much and gave Chloe a "Was that okay?" look. She nodded but gave me a silent "I got this." Then she handed Mom her manila folder. "Here's the evidence Amos, Ben, and I have found so far."

Mom took the folder from her and flipped through the first couple of pages. "Interesting."

Chloe didn't let up. "Most women blacksmiths made nails and smaller stuff. They had to learn the trade when men went off to fight. This is a part of history that deserves to be told. Right, Amos?"

"That's right," I said. "This year, we're asking all the questions we haven't heard asked before."

"Right," said Chloe. "About Black stories. Stories about women and girls and the queer community. Just because a bunch of mostly white men hammered history into one shape, it doesn't mean they got it right. Ms. Abernathy, please. This is important, not just for me but for everyone who comes to the LHP. I want to do something important, something no one's done before."

She didn't say it, but I know Chloe was thinking about how much it would mean to her dad. How maybe, for once, he wouldn't compare her to Cadence. How she could own a "first" for once in her life. A super big important first!

Mom slid Chloe's application into the folder. "I appreciate your passion, Chloe, I really do, but I'll have to talk this over with Brad. He hasn't taken on a junior apprentice in years, and I'll be honest—I don't know if he'd be comfortable bringing on a girl."

My eyebrow went up. "Isn't that a little sexist?"

"He's particular about accurately reflecting the era," Mom said, matching my eyebrow with her own. "And it's true that most women weren't blacksmiths. Even if you've found *some* evidence, I don't know if that'll be enough to sway Brad."

I'd been giving our "accuracy" a lot of thought, and what Mom said made me angry. "But we *don't* accurately reflect the era. Not really. We don't ever talk about race or slavery—everyone is welcome to volunteer, no matter the color of their skin. Why do only some identities matter when it comes to how we represent history?"

Mom shifted uncomfortably in her chair. "It's complicated, Amos. We do the best we can without offending people."

"Sometimes 'the best' isn't good enough," Chloe said. "We can do better. This is a chance for us to talk about the ugly truths we pretty much ignore at the LHP. The truth about my ancestors. About Illinois and slavery. What it took for a Black person to actually become free. Aren't we being historically inaccurate if we don't show what life was like for *everyone* back then?"

Mom's lips pursed. She was quiet for a while but finally said, "I'll see what he says."

Here's the thing about Chloe: She doesn't really wait for other people to get things done. So, that afternoon, she, Ben, and I took a detour down to the blacksmith's shop. It's a big barn-looking building, open on two sides for airflow. A huge, glassless window next to the furnace keeps the blacksmith from completely melting while he works. The shop always smells like bonfire, steam, and wet metal. But it was a chilly, breezy day, so I was ready for the heat.

Brad Pinot, our resident blacksmith, is a retired auto mechanic who, even at sixty-five, has boulders for biceps. But he's not all muscle. Over the winter, when the LHP is closed, he lets his ash-white beard creep down to his chest, and he looks a whole lot like buff Santa Claus. But when he's at work over fire and steaming metal all summer, he keeps his beard cropped close to his cheeks and chin.

When we showed up, he was nearing the end of a demonstration. We hung out in the back by a wall of tools I don't know the names of (Chloe does) and waited for the little old ladies from a nearby women's club to shuffle out. (I overheard one of them call Brad "cute"—*gross*.)

Chloe didn't hesitate. Without cracking a smile, she said, "I want to be your apprentice."

Brad put down his mallet and wiped his hands on his gray-brown apron. He smiled wide and, I swear, his pale cheeks rosied and his eyes twinkled.

"Oh, I don't think you want to apprentice here," he said. "It's a lot of hard work."

"I don't mind hard work."

Brad shifted his stance. "What about the homestead? Or the schoolhouse—I bet you'd make a great teacher."

Chloe's twin braids swung as she shook her head. "Not interested."

"Look, this is a dangerous work. I wouldn't want you to get hurt. Probably best—"

"I'm not afraid."

"Well, the blacksmith shop really isn't a place for a young woman," Brad said slowly, avoiding Chloe's gaze. He massaged the back of his neck. "What do your parents say? Have you talked to Ms. Abernathy about this?"

"My parents already signed off"—Chloe nodded—"and Ms. Abernathy said she'd have to talk to you."

"It didn't sound like she was against it," I added quickly.

Ben chimed in. "Chloe's been talking about blacksmithing ever since I met her. She'd be really good at it."

"And," Chloe said, stepping closer to the anvil, the blaze of the furnace rippling gold against her warm brown skin, "in case you're going to question it, we've already found historical proof that some women were blacksmiths."

"And *not* Wikipedia," I added.

Brad's whiskers twitched as he sniffled. "That may be true, but I'm not sure I'd be comfortable having a girl work here. It can be dangerous, even for boys, and with your long hair and your dress—there's a lot that could go wrong."

"I'll wear my hair in a tight bun. I've already looked into period-appropriate dresses that are flame resistant. And I'll be wearing an apron, same as you."

Brad was quiet. He tossed another log into the fire and it spit red. He stoked the flames noncommittally with an iron rod before turning back to us. "I'll need to think about it."

Chloe smiled, but only a little. "I'd appreciate that." She stuck out her hand, and a smirk split Brad's lips. He took Chloe's hand and shook it—hard. Everything up to Chloe's shoulder trembled, but she didn't let go.

So, we're waiting to see what Brad and Mom decide. If I were Brad, I'd be impressed. Chloe clearly knows what she wants, and she isn't afraid to do something that hasn't been done before. I mean, I'd take her on as my apprentice.

Okay. Sooooooo, remember how I said I have NEWS? You are never going to believe it. I'm still not sure *I do*.

Freaking Ben Oglevie.

So, here's what happened. Chloe had to go straight to a family thing after volunteering on Sunday, so her dad picked her up instead of Mom and me driving her home. That meant Ben and I were alone for a while, which happens sometimes, but not that often. Since March, it really has been the three of us against the world (well, at least against Meredith Simmons and Mindy Liu . . . ugh).

It was freezing out, so Ben and I were in the Chickaree Café, which is attached to the main visitors' center, drinking hot chocolate. He was acting weird. Looking over his shoulder a lot, leg twitching.

And then he said this. "I want to show you something." He slid his phone across the table. A screenshot from some website. A poem.

For Reuben and Charles have married two girls,
But Billy has married a boy.
The girls he had tried on every side,
But none he could get to agree;
All was in vain, he went home again,
And since that he's married to Natty.

I laughed out loud when I got to the end and (half) jokingly said, "Did you write that?"

He blurted, "What? No!"

"Who did?" I said, remembering I was supposed to be backing off, because HE'S NOT INTO YOU, AMOS.

But then he grinned, and his fingers wrapped tightly around his cup. "Guess."

This felt like flirting, but it couldn't be flirting. And I

was *not* going to fake flirt. So, I said, "I have no idea."

Ben pulled his cup close to his chest, and his chin leaned forward. He whispered, "Abraham Lincoln."

"No way." I was actually in shock. "You made that up."

"Swear I didn't." He talked faster. His voice got louder. "I got bored the other night, and since we only have a week before our proposal is due, I was doing some research at home—"

"For real? Didn't you say your parents would freak?" I sipped my hot chocolate, licking away the foamy bits from my lip.

"They don't *usually* check my phone, and I'm tired of only looking stuff up when I'm at your house," he said. "Anyway, I found this article about how Lincoln might have been gay. He wrote this poem when he was young, before he was president or the Civil War started."

"Oh my god," I said, scanning the poem again. "Could you even imagine if Lincoln was queer?"

His chair creaked as he repositioned himself. "After everything we've been finding, yeah, I think I could imagine it. And I can't help but think, What if Lincoln grew up today? Would he have had a First Man instead of a Mary Todd Lincoln? What if society hadn't made him think he was wrong, that that poem wasn't a silly, stupid thing but, like, okay?"

I gave my cup a swirl. "We know, don't we? He could

have married Natty. He wouldn't need to hide."

The table started to jitter. Ben's leg was thumping faster than a baby rabbit's heartbeat. He lowered his voice. "I don't want to hide."

Suddenly my stomach was hugging my heart. "Hide what?"

"You know what, Amos."

"No," I said because I'd already ruled out that option. "I don't. You haven't actually told me anything, and I'm tired of playing guessing games."

Ben exhaled. His sweet, cocoa-y breath wafted across to me. "Amos, I—I think I'm not exactly straight."

Inside my head: OHMYGODOHMYGODOHMY-GOD.

Outside my head: "Oh."

"I'm tired of so many things, Amos. I'm just tired." He looked up at me. Even his eyes were hot chocolate now. "I guess what I'm trying to say is . . . would you want to hang out sometime?"

"Aren't we doing that now?" I asked, trying to laugh off the awkwardness of it all. My brain was still processing the words "not exactly straight."

Another over the shoulder glance, and then Ben leaned across the table to whisper, "I mean, like, not while we're volunteering. Just us."

My mouth opened before I thought it through. "You

can come over tomorrow. Mom's making lasagna, and it's usually not terrible. Mr. Blake will be there, too."

He shook his head. "Nothing against your mom or her lasagna, but I was thinking, I don't know, maybe we could like go see a movie or something." He blushed cranberry crimson.

That's when I realized what he was actually saying.

I leaned across the table. "Benjamin Oglevie, are you trying to ask me out?"

I didn't think it was possible to turn a shade redder, but his cheeks found a way. "Uh, I mean, I don't know," he said. By then his leg was jackhammering under the table so bad I had to pick up my hot chocolate. "Would you want that?"

I couldn't believe this was happening. There had to be a catch, but I found myself saying, "I wouldn't not want that."

His left eye squinted closed. "Can you not double negative me right now?"

I needed to know, plain and simple, what the heck was going on. I leaned back in my chair, taking my hot chocolate with me. "I didn't think you felt that way about me."

"I do," he said, "it's just not easy for me to say it. To do any of this. But I want to, and I really don't know what I'm doing."

"So . . . what *are* you doing?" I was turning into a shaken-up two liter of Coke.

He looked up and his eyes were a mudslide. "Amos, I'm trying to figure that out."

His phone buzzed. He flipped it right side up. "My brother Nathan. He's here."

And then he just watched me. And I watched him watching me. It was this weird staring contest that could have gone on forever.

I set my cup on the table. "That new Marvel movie looks all right."

He smiled. "*Shang-Chi and the Legend of the Ten Rings*? I've heard good things."

"Might be worth our time."

"Friday night?"

"I'll have to check with Mom, but, yeah, Friday."

ALBERT. This is quite possibly the greatest day of my life. Or soon to be SECOND greatest day of my life. On Friday I'm going on a not-*not* date with a boy who doesn't not like me and may not not be gay who I definitely don't not like back.

Life is so weird. And great. Great and weird.

Freaking Ben Oglevie.

Thanks for listening.

Your friend,

Amos Abernathy

16

Logan Schoolhouse
Saturday, August 13, 2022—11:46 a.m.

Visitors file out of the schoolhouse. Chloe and I hang back while the other volunteers follow behind, giggling and skipping down the hill to their next assignments. Soon as we're out the door, I lead her around the side of the building. I've had a good fifteen minutes to stare at nothing and stew.

"How long have you known Ben was coming today?"

"It's not like that, Amos."

"You're supposed to be *my* best friend, Chloe. Not his. When were you going to tell me?"

Her lips press together. "Look, it's not what you think. Ben and I haven't been going behind your back or anything. He showed up this morning out of nowhere."

"Just like that?"

"I swear. He was waiting for me at the general store when I started my shift."

I search her eyes. "What did he say to you?"

"Well, um, what do you know?"

I hand her the note. "That I'm supposed to tell *you* if I want to talk to him."

"You got the note." She sounds relieved. "I was worried you already saw him."

"What would be so bad about that? Why doesn't he just come talk to me? Why did he even drag you into it?"

"Hey, it's not like I asked for this." She backs up a step. "*This* is why he's nervous. He's afraid you'll bite his head off."

"Oh come on! I'm not *that* scary." My hands fly into the air. "It's not like I'm going to beat him up."

Her eyes widen. *"Ummmmm. Suuure."*

"Fine." I simmer. "Maybe I wouldn't have the best reaction."

A hot gust blows over us. I try to ignore the queasiness in my gut. I need some water.

Chloe kicks my shoe. "So . . . *do* you want to talk to him?"

Before I can answer, Ms. Wiseman rounds the corner. "Thought I heard you two over here. Everything all right?"

"We're good." I adjust my haversack. "Sorry I got weird in there."

"Weird?" She pulls out her pocket watch. "Ugh, I'm running behind, which means the same for you two. And, Amos, don't you have the battle coming up?"

"Yeah," I say, "What time is it?"

"Just before noon," says Ms. Wiseman. "All right, I really need to get along. I'll see you both later this afternoon. Good luck, Amos!"

Ms. Wiseman nearly skips down the hill.

Chloe squints back at me. "So, what should I tell Ben?"

"Nothing," I say, then quickly backtrack. "Actually, no. Tell him if he really wants to talk to me, he needs to do it himself."

17

Friday, November 5, 2021

Dear Albert,

I have so much good news to share!

Yesterday, Chloe, Ben, Ms. Wiseman, and I submitted our formal proposal for the Forgotten Voices exhibit at the Living History Park. We put together four typed pages, single spaced, summarizing everything we'd found about people who were most likely LGBTQ+ in nineteenth-century America, plus a bibliography and our binder of evidence. The part I'm most proud of is the section titled "Why This Exhibit Matters." Here's a little bit of what I wrote:

> *The Forgotten Voices exhibit is an important and neces-*
> *sary addition to the Chickaree County Living History*
> *Park for many reasons. To start, history is complex*
> *and without the stories of underrepresented voices,*
> *we have an incomplete understanding of the way life*

actually worked back then—we silence the stories of people from so many identities and instead privilege the voices of straight, white cisgender men and women (but mostly men). Beyond historical accuracy, it's important for all people, and especially for people in the LGBTQ+ community, to know their history and celebrate the predecessors who blazed the trails for the roads we've paved today. LGBTQ+ people have been a part of American history since before the country was founded, but little has been done to recognize their contributions. This exhibit is important for all LGBTQ+ people, and will inspire them to be proud of their identity and their history and to continue making a difference in the world.

If I'm being honest, Albert, Ms. Wiseman helped us a lot with the wording and the editing, but the ideas are all ours. I kind of can't believe we actually did it. If Ben hadn't seen that gay couple, if he hadn't asked that question, we wouldn't have this proposal that could create an exhibit that changes lives!

I know this might sound weird or selfish, but, excited as I was about turning in the proposal to Mom, I still felt like something was missing. When she took the binder, it felt like I was giving something away, not like I'd finally found something. Does that make any sense?

"Amazing work, you three. I'm not promising anything," she said, leafing through the binder, "but this is a very impressive proposal, and we haven't received all that many submissions, even with the deadline on Sunday."

There was only one other proposal that mattered to me. "Did Meredith Simmons and Mindy Liu turn theirs in?"

"Not yet. Mr. Simmons mentioned Meredith and Mindy have been working very hard on it . . . but I'd be shocked if they handed in something like this." She set the binder down on her desk. "Still, I am a little curious to see how much further they got beyond that coupon."

"You can't go with their proposal, Mom. Who cares about *shoes*?"

"To be fair," Chloe said, "I do like shoes."

GLARE. "But not *their* shoes."

"Amos, it's not up to just me," Mom said, saving Chloe from my laser vision. "The whole board has to agree."

I've got to say, Albert, that does worry me. The *whole* board, which is mostly made up of old straight white cis men. I hope they can see that the lives of *actual human beings* are more important than footwear.

No matter what, I'm proud of what we've accomplished and what we've learned. Ben, Chloe, and I, and maybe even Ms. Wiseman, have changed since we started this project. I think we all smile a bit more than we used to.

After we turned in our proposal, Mom pulled Chloe

aside, but I sort of heard everything they said. I'm a highly skilled dropper of eaves. (It runs in the family.)

"It took some convincing," Mom said, "but Brad Pinot has agreed to let you apprentice on a trial basis. One week with him to start, and then a final decision will be made."

Chloe screamed and wrapped her arms around Mom's neck. "Thank you, thank you, thank you!" She let Mom go. "You won't regret this. I'm going to be the best blacksmith this park has ever seen."

Mom straightened out the front of her dress where Chloe's explosion of joy had wrinkled it. "I'm counting on it. You kids really have done some incredible work this fall. I'm very proud."

Obviously, Ben and I are THRILLED for Chloe.

Ben and I—then there's us.

So, remember how I told you about him asking me to go see a movie? Well, we went tonight. We sat in the back all the way in the top row, so no one was behind us. For a Friday night, it wasn't very full in the theater, and neither of us saw anyone we recognized. I was majorly relieved—after accidentally saying his name at church, I could only imagine what people would think if they saw us at a movie together.

We shared a popcorn and got two drinks—he got Cherry Coke and I got Sprite. For a while, we stayed close to the edges of the popcorn bucket, making sure our fingers didn't touch, but once it happened by accident, it kept happening.

And then our knees were touching, and fireworks were going off in my chest, and I wondered if Ben had the same thing going on inside him, and I figured he must because he didn't pull away.

Halfway through the movie, we put the popcorn bucket on the floor because it was cold and mostly kernels. The way we shifted to put it on the floor meant our knees weren't touching and our fingers couldn't "accidently" bump into each other anymore.

It took me longer to muster up the courage than I'd like to admit, but I eventually put my hand on the armrest between us. At first Ben didn't do anything, and I thought he was too into the movie to notice I was making a move (the movie was pretty awesome). But then he rested his left foot on his right knee and scooted a little closer to me. Then his hand was on his left knee, less than an inch from mine. I watched all of this happen out of the corner of my eye, my heart ricocheting around my throat. I stretched out my fingers and closed the gap between us. His fingers twitched, and then our pinkies wrapped around each other, then our ring fingers.

That was it, but it was AMAZING. I do not remember how the movie ended.

The lights came up way too fast and as soon as they did, we let go of each other. I didn't realize how hard I'd been holding on to him. With just those two fingers.

"Not as good as *Black Panther*," Ben said as we left the theater, as if everything was totally normal, "but I don't think anything will ever compare to that."

"Um, *Infinity War?*" I said, trying to match his chill.

He shrugged. "It was kind of predictable."

I shoved him. "*You're* predictable."

I couldn't have said anything further from the truth.

Mom was picking me up, and one of Ben's brothers was coming for him. They both knew when the movie was supposed to end but neither of them was there yet. It was cold, misting a little bit, but we waited outside anyway. Our breath became little clouds.

I didn't want the not-not date to end. I would have given anything to go back to our fingers wrapped around each other, so I held my arms open and said, "Say goodbye before our rides get here?"

He smiled. "Yeah, sure."

When he walked into my arms, warmth bubbled up from my stomach and I held on to him tight. The edges of our ears rubbed up against each other, and I don't know what came over me, but as we pulled away . . . I kissed him on the cheek. Well, I *tried* to kiss him on the cheek, but it was more like my lips slipped against his skin for half a second.

Albert, I thought I was going to die right there, in front of Cinemaplex 12.

But all Ben said was, "Oh."

Even in the near dark of the movie theater parking lot I could tell he was blushing something fierce. What I couldn't tell was if that was a good or a bad thing.

Before I could ask, headlights turned on us and we took an extra step apart.

"My brother," he said, fidgeting with his jacket zipper. "I'll see you tomorrow, okay?"

Nathan's car came to a stop.

"I had fun tonight," I said.

He smiled. "Me, too."

Mom showed up a second after they pulled away, and the first thing she asked was, "So how was the date?"

"It wasn't a date, Mom!" I hadn't realized she could tell I liked him.

I'd never admit it to her, but Mom's right, Albert. That was so totally not *not* a date. It was a *date* date just like he *like* likes my face. And you know what I'm realizing? That maybe you don't have to call something a *thing* for it to be. Not sure if that makes sense, but it feels like it does. At least to me.

Anyway, I'm excited to see Ben tomorrow. Now if only I could fall asleep.

Good night, Albert.

Your friend,

Amos Abernathy

18

★ ★ ★

Logan Schoolhouse
Saturday, August 13, 2022—11:55 a.m.

At the base of the hill, Chloe and I part ways.

"I'll see you later," she says. "Don't be mad, okay?"

"I'm not mad. I'm frustrated."

She shrugs. "Maybe it's a good thing the battle's up next, then? You'll have something to distract you for a little while? Drums make you happy!"

Fine. She wins. I smile. "If you hear tales about a berserk drummer boy who took down an entire regiment of Confederate soldiers with just his drumsticks and a broken heart, you'll be the one to blame."

She presses a hand to her chest. "My stars! I do look forward to hearing those tales."

Chloe heads toward the Wakefield House, and I about-face to make for the fort. I've taken a few steps when Darren comes up behind me. His reddish beard glistens with sweat.

"Amos, hey!" He shoves his glasses up the bridge of his

nose. "Perfect timing. I was just heading over to the fort. Walk with me?"

"Sure." Nothing against Darren, but I'm not really in the mood for company right now.

One, two, three beats of silence. Then Darren says, "Is everything all right, Amos? You seem off."

"I'm fine. I just—I feel like I can't catch up with today. It's all happening so fast."

Darren's hand catches my arm. "Slow down a sec, then," he says. "I want you and the boys to run a few drills before the battle, but we've got a minute."

"Okay."

Darren's face softens. His hand on my arm goes from a grab to a gentle squeeze.

"Amos, I've known you a long time," he says. "Even before your mom and I started dating, you know I've always been in your corner. You can talk to me if something's up."

Of all the men Mom could date, I would have thought Darren Blake would be the best choice. The *perfect* choice. But sometimes mixing these worlds—home and school and music and the LHP—it's a lot.

"I'm fine."

Darren nods. "Okay."

I follow a half step behind, thoughts of Ben and three o'clock and the GSA kids showing up early and Chloe (sort of) lying to me crashing around in my head like sneakers in a dryer.

Darren snaps me back to reality. "You know, it took me a long time to work up the courage to talk to your mom, and even more for me to ask her out."

Oh my god. This is not happening. I clear my throat. "Don't get me wrong, I'm cool with you two dating now, but . . . we don't need to talk about it."

Darren chuckles. "My point isn't about us dating, I promise."

"That was a weird way to start, then."

"That only better serves my point." He laughs. "Us men, we don't always know how to communicate. Words get jumbled, feelings don't match what comes out of our mouths. You know?"

"That's some binary thinking," I grumble. "I'm pretty sure all people have trouble communicating."

Darren nods. "That's fair. Then I'll only speak for my experience and what I've found to be true for other men I know. Okay?"

"I guess."

We turn down the path toward the grassy field and the fort. Gravel crunches beneath our feet.

"Amos, you have a gift with words. You have this way of speaking honestly and openly about how you feel. It's incredible, and it's been amazing to watch you grow. How authentically you live. Not everyone has that."

I kick a small rock into the grass.

"A lot of men, myself included, were taught to keep our emotions in check. Talking about how I feel, being honest about it? Never been easy for me. And when you're already struggling with your feelings, it's even harder to express what's going on inside. With me so far?"

"Yeah."

Darren inhales. "Well, when you add romantic feelings into the mix, it compounds everything. What should be easy to say can become impossible, or it comes out all wrong. And when you're insecure or afraid . . ."

Hold up. "What did Mom tell you?"

"Oh." Darren turns, squinting into the sun. "Nothing much. Just mentioned you might be having some boy troubles is all."

My cheeks redden. I can't remember the last time a man talked to me like this. Like a dad. "So, you *are* talking about Ben?"

"I'm talking about *you*, Amos." Darren holds a visor of fingers to his forehead. "Sure, Ben has his issues, that's clear, but you're the one I care about. Not that I don't care about Ben. It's just—you get what I'm saying, don't you?"

All the sudden, my feet become very interesting. "Yeah,

I hear you." Huh. The laces on my left shoe have come loose. "But I'm not scared. I'm . . . I'm sad. I'm angry. And so freaking confused."

"Uh-huh."

"How do you talk to someone who hurt you, who you want to punch in the face, when you still care about them?"

Darren's hand rests on my shoulder. "Amos, if there was a guidebook for these things, it would be up there with the Bible on the bestseller list. Best I can offer is trust your gut and be honest, for better or worse, whether you're feeling anger, sadness, confusion, or all three. You are one of the most passionate, genuine kids I've ever taught. You'll find a way to say what's in your heart."

"Yeah?"

"Yeah," Darren says, his hand sliding up to my neck, tugging me forward. "Now come on. We've got a battle to fight."

19

Saturday, November 6, 2021

Dear Albert,

When I was six years old, I learned that life has a way of balancing itself. It's like, whenever something good happens, something equally terrible has to happen right after—like there can't be too much of something positive or negative. And the bigger the good thing that happens, the bigger the disaster that comes next.

My sixth Christmas was the best—Mom, Dad, and I spent the entire day watching movies and baking cookies and opening presents. I got everything I asked for and then some. Legos, video games, an Abraham Lincoln coloring book. But what I wanted more than anything in the whole world was a vintage tea set.

You heard me right, Albert. I was obsessed with making tea and having tea parties. I didn't invite my teddy bear or anything, but the whole process of steeping the crushed leaves in boiled water—something about it fascinated me.

So, Mom and Dad bought me this gorgeous ceramic tea set they'd found in an antique shop. It came with four mint-green cups with delicate handles, glossy and silky to the touch, and a matching teapot. They also got me an electric kettle because they didn't want me using the stove, and I insisted on making the tea ALL BY MYSELF. More than play with my new Lego mansion or new Pokémon game, all I wanted to do was brew every tea we had in the house, and that's what we did, all Christmas long.

It was the best, Albert. The. Best. I was on top of the freaking world.

And then came January seventh. Usually there's nothing special about January seventh—it's just another day. That year it was another *Wednesday*. I went to school, Mom went to work at the LHP, and Dad went off to plow early in the morning like he usually did during snowy weather.

I came home.

Mom came home.

And Dad didn't come home.

And he didn't come home.

And he didn't come home.

It happened at 6:42 p.m. just outside the grocery on Jefferson and Main. Dad had dropped off the plow and was headed home in our Toyota when a drunk driver came out of nowhere and T-boned him on the driver's side. They said it happened fast. They said he didn't feel anything. They said he wouldn't have been in pain.

That was the worst day of my life. The worst year of my life, Albert. I thought Mom and I wouldn't survive losing him. I still miss him every day, but it doesn't hurt quite as badly as it used to. We've learned to deal, and Mom's even started dating again. She and Mr. Blake officially started dating a couple of weeks ago (he wants me to call him Darren now!!!), which is weird. Good, but weird.

I should have remembered, Albert. I should have remembered that life balances good things with bad.

I lost Ben today.

That sounds like he's dead—he's not dead. But I can't decide if he needs to be rescued or if I want to punch him.

Here's what happened. Last night, we went on our not-date and saw the movie and then we hugged, and I sort of kissed him on the cheek, if you can really call that a kiss, and then we got picked up and went on our separate ways and I felt great and all was right in the world.

Cut to today, the last day of the junior volunteering season. I was excited to see Ben, but I also hated the fact that we wouldn't be seeing each other all the time anymore.

But he never showed. I double- and triple-checked to make sure he was on the schedule. When I asked Mom if she'd heard from him, she said she hadn't. She'd even called to check on him, but no one answered.

That's when an all too familiar dread knotted in my stomach. Hot and cold chills actually ran up and down my back, just like they write about in books, and I thought I was going to throw up because all I could think was I'd had too many good things happen to me and the universe was balancing itself and Ben Oglevie was dead.

I texted him as soon as I got home (Mom makes me leave my cell phone behind even though EVERY OTHER KID KEEPS THEIRS IN THEIR HAVERSACK OR BASKET, but WHATEVER).

He didn't respond.

And he didn't respond.

And he didn't respond.

So, I called him, because that's what you do in emergencies and you think your friend who is also the boy you like might be dead.

After it rang for way too long, a voice I didn't recognize answered the phone.

"Hi, Amos?"

"Uh, hi," I said. "Is Ben there?"

"This is Mr. Oglevie, Ben's dad." The knot cinching my stomach gave a sickening tug. "He's . . . not available."

"Is he all right? Did something happen? He was supposed to volunteer today, but he never—"

"He's fine," his dad said, "but he won't be volunteering anymore."

"Why not?"

"His mom and I decided it's not the . . . environment we want for our son."

"What does that mean?" I couldn't help myself. I don't usually talk back to parents.

Mr. Oglevie hesitated, then cleared his throat. "His mother and I think the relationships he's developing are influencing him to make poor decisions."

That's when I realized what was really going on. "Are—are you saying that because of me?"

Mr. Oglevie was quiet for a long time. My heart jammed up in my throat while I waited for him to say something. My eyes teared up even though I bit my lip. I wiped them fast because I didn't want him to hear me crying.

Finally, he said, "We're sorry, Amos, but our family has certain beliefs, and we all know Ben will be better off if he has different influences in his life."

Different *influences*, Albert. As if *I* did this to Ben. As if him liking me is *my* fault.

"What does Ben think?" I asked.

"We *all* think this is for the best. I'm sorry, Amos."

And then he hung up. I couldn't bring myself to call back. I felt so . . . empty.

Mom walked in and found me crying on the couch. I felt like such a baby, but I didn't stop her when she pulled me into her arms. She asked if I was all right, and I didn't want to tell her the truth, but it came out in fractured bits until the whole thing had spilled onto the floor like an upturned puzzle. I don't think even Mom could see the whole picture, which might be why she made the irrational decision to take my phone, dial Ben's number into her own, and call the Oglevies.

At first, I was mortified, and I tried to yank the phone from her, but she had a fiery rage in her eyes. "No, Amos. *No.* This is wrong." I stopped trying to stop her and wiped snot from my upper lip.

"Hello, is this Mr. Oglevie?" she said in a voice like a fizzing-to-burst two liter of soda. "Hi, this is Hannah Abernathy, Amos's mom."

There was a brief moment where I held my breath as, I assume, Mr. Oglevie responded to Mom. Her face squinched like it does when a migraine is coming on. "Look, Doug, I don't think you understand what's really going on here. My son is a mess because of what you said to him. Not only were you *completely* out of line, you are depriving not only Amos, but *your* son, of one of his best friends.

"And as far as *influences* go, I promise you Amos is one of the best influences your son will ever have. Amos is kind, motivated, assertive, determined, and I couldn't be prouder of the young man he's becoming. But if you think for even a second that my son could've possibly *influenced* your son into thinking he has feelings for mine, then you are sorely mistaken. There was no *influence*. There was birth and brain chemistry and hormones, and, Doug, you need to get with the twenty-first century."

She finally inhaled, and I thought she might be done, but, nope, she just kept on steamrolling. "And if you ever, *ever* speak to my son that way again, I swear I will show up at your front door and you'll see what hell looks like. Our boys—your *son*—deserve better than your primitive, backward, abusive way of thinking. I hope Ben knows that he is beautiful and perfect and worthy just as he is, and"— her voice went up a notch—"AND IF HE'S LISTENING, HE ALWAYS HAS A SAFE PLACE HERE."

Then she hung up, and she looked wiped out, but there was also this terrifying, wild energy around her. Her gaze narrowed on me. "No one treats my son that way and gets away with it. *No one*."

I've never been prouder *or* more horrified of Mom, Albert.

Her arms folded around me. "Amos, I'm so sorry you had to experience that. That man is a bigot." She sighed. "Poor Ben."

I worry about Ben, too, Albert. A lot. What he must be thinking, about us, about himself. I keep trying to text him, but nothing comes back. Mom thinks his parents took his phone away.

So, there you go. Life balanced itself once more.

One night Christmas, the next night car accident. Good and bad. Together and alone.

But I can't shake the last thing Mr. Oglevie said to me. *We all know this is for the best.*

We *all* know. He couldn't have meant Ben, too. No way he changed his mind about us. *He* asked *me* to go see the movie. There were fireworks. There's just no way he didn't feel them, too. Right?

But what if he was just being nice? What if instead of knowing for sure he *like* likes me he figured out he's *not* into me? Maybe this isn't just about his parents. Maybe he really *doesn't* want to see me again. Maybe I super overdid it with that mega-fail sort-of kiss on the cheek and I *am* the reason he's gone.

I'm the reason.

Albert, I really messed up. I just honestly don't know how.

I don't know what to think anymore.

I'm sad, Albert.

Your friend,

Amos Abernathy

20

Battlefield
Saturday, August 13, 2022—12:02 p.m.

Nearly a hundred men, boys, and a handful of women in gray and blue are camped out inside the pine fort that opens onto the big field in the center of the park. The fort is usually open to visitors, and the field is where we play cricket, but today it's our stage for a rerun from America's Civil War.

Darren leads me around a trio of other beardy men who smell like nasty socks, past the central bonfire, and around to the lookout tower where Noah Barringer and Chase Pfeiffer wait. Noah could pass for a fourth grader, he's so short, but he just finished eighth grade like me. For as hot as it is, his tanned olive skin isn't even glistening with sweat. Lucky him. Chase is the exact opposite—tall, skinny, and sweaty. His white cheeks are bright red. He takes off his hat and waves it at me and then fans himself. He'll be a sophomore at Chickaree High School. I'm friendly with the guys, but we don't really hang outside of volunteering or practice.

"We've got about thirty minutes before showtime," Darren says. "Let's run through everything one more time."

Chase scratches the ridge of acne along his pale cheek. "We've got this, Mr. Blake. We know what we're doing."

"Don't get cocky," Darren says, and then someone calls his name, asking about a bayonet. He walks away, wagging his finger, telling us to get started and that when he gets back, we'd better sound like "the real deal."

Noah twirls his stick in the air and catches it without any effort. "We'll sound *better* than the real deal."

"Wasn't sure you were coming," Chase says, frowning at me.

"Sorry," I say. "It's been a weird day. Too many things going on."

Chase nods. "It's all good. Your drum and sticks are over there. Spare Union jacket is hung up on the banister for you. And you can throw your haversack under the stairs with ours."

I toss my haversack on top of theirs. Then I fit my arms through the thick navy-blue jacket and lower the leather straps of the military drum around my head. The familiar heaviness feels good. I'm in control here. No Mom or Ben or performance to worry about.

"All set?" Noah asks, flipping his rosewood stick again.

160

A fresh trickle of sweat slides down my face. "Let's do this."

For the next twenty minutes or so, we run through the twenty-six rudiments Civil War drummer boys had to memorize. Reveille and march. The steady rat-tat-tat of the call to battle. I'm not sure we sound like the "real deal," but we're in sync and our rhythms are good. Well, sometimes Noah falls behind, but Chase and me play louder to cover up his flubs. The guys and I have totally got this.

At five minutes to one, Darren hollers for the Union soldiers to form ranks while the Confederate soldiers are led out the back of the fort. When the reenactment starts, they'll come around the south end of the field, near New Hope Church, and assault the fort from the front.

Darren reminds Chase and me to grab rifles before we get in place. This is the first year Mom is letting us actually join the battle. I'm so freaking excited. All our gear in hand, I lead Chase and Noah up the steep wooden steps of the watchtower and down the rampart. The low wall of logs reaches just above my waist. Poor Noah can barely see over the top.

"Lots of people came out today," Noah says, leaning his rifle against the fort wall.

Thin ropes staked along the edges of the field mark off where we'll do battle. Behind the ropes, families and couples sit on blankets with picnic baskets. There's got to be hundreds of people here to watch. And—oh my god. The Gay Cerberus. I duck behind Chase and the confidence I'd felt building washes away. Cassidy, Azul, Kevin, and a few more of the GSA kids are waving their arms and shouting my name like I'm a pop star. I should be pumped, all these eyes on us, my friends cheering me on, but now I've got Ben and Albert on my mind again. Chase gives me a weird look, so I turn back to the field and I imagine Albert standing alone in the grass. Not just a soldier. Just a *person* surrounded by other people laughing, cheering. Eating cotton candy and drinking lemonade. Picnic blanket after picnic blanket of families sitting around like they're waiting for fireworks on the Fourth of July. And something slips out of place in my gut. For the first time ever, all of this battle reenactment stuff makes me a little sad. Hollow. The noise of the crowd fills up that space and it feels wrong.

The LHP is open most days of the year. Why does the largest crowd turn out only to watch us pretend to kill each other?

That's all kinds of messed up. And now it's making *me* feel all messed up. More than I already do.

At the far end of the field, across from where the guys and I stand with our drums, our elbows bent at the ready, the Confederate soldiers form their ranks. The lilt of a fife sends an electric charge crackling through the air.

Over the noise of the crowd, Darren shouts an order

162

to the Union soldiers. They hold their guns steady, eyes pointed down their barrels. The field goes suddenly quiet. It's eerie. The dull hum of insects fills my ears. My sticks shake over my drum. I never get nervous like this, but I can't steady my hands.

Suddenly, Darren lifts his saber and shouts. Chase and Noah immediately fall into unison rhythm, but I'm a beat behind them. *Get it together, Amos.*

A cannon blasts. My fingers clench tighter around my sticks.

The battle is on.

21

Saturday, December 11, 2021

Dear Albert,

You probably already noticed, but it's been about a month since I last wrote to you. There's something I've been dreading telling you, but I feel like I owe it to you, even if what I've got to say totally sucks. Remember before how I said life has a way of balancing the good with the bad? Well, right now we're on a downhill collision course from bad to absolutely terrible.

No, no one died, so we're not anywhere close to how low I know life can take you, but I'm pretty miserable.

I haven't heard a word from Ben. I thought he might try to stay in touch with Chloe at least, but she hasn't heard from him either. He's just gone, and now we have this Ben-shaped puzzle piece missing, like Chloe and I were always supposed to be a trio and we just didn't know it until he showed up.

That sounds bad. Chloe is and always will be my best

friend—I don't need someone else around for that to be true. I guess, without Ben, my life feels incomplete. *I* feel incomplete. And I know Chloe misses him, too. With so many older brothers, Ben understood what she goes through always trying to live up to Cadence.

Now it's like bad news is contagious. A couple of weeks ago, Brad Pinot, henceforth known as Evil Santa, decided he's not going to take on *any* blacksmithing apprentices this upcoming year. Mom was the one who broke the news to Chloe.

"He thinks it's too much of a liability," Mom said. "I can't make him take you on if he feels it would be unsafe."

"But I promise I'll be careful! And my parents already said they'll sign off on whatever."

"I'm sorry, Chloe, but I think this is for the best. Maybe we can talk about it again next year, when you're a little older."

Mom must feel bad about the whole thing, because she let Chloe choose from all the other apprenticeships without even filling out an application. She settled on the stables. (Or, as she put it: "No way am I going to end up at the schoolhouse or the homestead. I'm not letting Evil Santa think he's won!")

And that brings me to what I've been dreading telling you, Albert.

I've failed you. Your memory, your bravery, your courage.

And not just you—I've failed our entire queer community.

A few nights ago, Mom knocked on my door. "You got a sec?"

I'd been reading more of Walt Whitman's poetry—I couldn't decide which poems we'd probably want to highlight in the exhibit. There are so many good ones! I closed the book and sat up on the bed, and right away I knew it was bad because Mom didn't say whatever it was from the doorway. She came in, plopped down, and pulled both legs onto my bed.

I really didn't want to know, but I asked anyway. "What's going on?"

"The board has been reviewing the applications for the exhibit, and they are extremely impressed with the time and effort everyone put into their proposals." At that point, I thought life might be righting itself—that everything that had gone wrong with Ben would go right for the Forgotten Voices exhibit.

Mom went on, "It turns out the competition for the exhibit is steeper than anticipated. Obviously, word has gotten around about various proposals—you and Meredith Simmons have both been trying to get the word out. So have the Chickaree County Women's Society and the First Methodist Church down on Woodchuck Road—"

"Mom, just tell me. Did they accept our proposal? Who won?"

Her eyebrows rose as she closely examined my comforter. "Amos, I hate having to tell you this, but you deserve to know the truth. Mr. Simmons contacted the board with a complaint."

I snorted. "What? He hates gay people now, too?"

"Not exactly," said Mom. "He argued that the board shouldn't accept proposals from board members or their immediate family because of potential bias or favoritism. That it would be unfair to the community members who don't have a connection to the board."

"But that's ridiculous!" I said. "He can't tell the board what to do, and besides, he knows you're super critical. If you knew our proposal sucked, you wouldn't even try convincing the board to accept it."

She nodded. "I know that, and you know that, but part of this is about perception. I tried to reason with him. I offered to step down from the selection process. But the board agreed with Mr. Simmons that they would not be able to remain impartial given that I'm your mother."

I jumped off my bed. Until then I'd never *actually* wanted to punch a wall. "That's totally ridiculous!"

"I know, sweetie, believe me. I was furious. I *am* furious."

I crossed my arms to keep my walls safe. "Mr. Simmons can't tell the board what to do. He doesn't have that kind of power."

She sighed. "In a roundabout way, he does, Amos."

167

I wasn't expecting that. I sat back down on the bed. "How?"

Mom's fingers were massaging the base of her neck. "He threatened to pull all his funding from the Living History Park if we didn't 'avoid blatant nepotism.'" She couldn't even look at me as she said it.

"Are you kidding me?" My insides were shattering, but I jumped off the bed and started pacing. "So, the board is going to let Mr. Simmons bully them because they're afraid of losing a little money?"

"It's not a little money, Amos. The Simmons family funds a huge portion of the LHP. Without them, we'd have to shut down operations almost immediately. Never mind the fact that some board members truly think it's the right thing to do."

"What do *you* think?"

"Of course I think it's ridiculous, but we can't lose the Simmonses' donation. We just . . . we don't have the revenue to cover our costs. We're talking about my *job*, Amos. Our livelihood."

I kept pacing. "Did they even read our proposal? Do they have any idea how hard Ms. Wiseman, Chloe, Ben, and I worked on this?"

Her head hung. "Mr. Simmons got to the board before proposals were distributed for review, but many of them knew about it. I know Jerry Winfield was eager to read it.

And I read it, cover to cover." When she finally looked up at me, her eyes were glassy. "It was such a professional and important proposal. I would have been honored to select it. I am so sorry."

I wanted to be angry. I am now. But right then, I just felt numb. "Did they decide on an exhibit yet?" I was pretty sure I knew where this was headed. All I had to do was follow the money.

"They did."

"And?"

"I'm sorry, Amos." She sighed. "Shoes of the Nineteenth Century will open in March."

There you go, Albert. No exhibit for me, no apprenticeship for Chloe, no Ben for us, and no Ben allowed to be Ben (unless he was lying to me about everything).

It's all a mess.

I'm so sorry, Albert. I hope you can forgive me. I really thought we could share your story.

Amos

22

Battlefield
Saturday, August 13, 2022—12:37 p.m.

After the first cannon blast, the Confederate infantry storms up the hillside, where pockets of smoke are planted in the grass. As Chase, Noah, and I beat our drums, Union soldiers fire and soldiers in gray fall. Dusty white clouds billow up from the field. Some of the reenactors have packets of "blood" waiting in their cheeks. When the time's right, they chomp down and red runs over their chins. With the right flailing, a reenactor can sell a pretty cringe-worthy death. (At least, I hope that's why our audience is cringing.)

At the far end of the field, the Confederate drummer boys—Tommy Graves, Braydon Wozniak, and Hal Harris—mirror us. While we drummer boys keep a steady beat, everyone else runs amok. Of course, it's well-choreographed chaos. We've all been practicing for the past two weeks. Except five minutes into the battle, two of the Confederate drummer boys (Tommy and Hal) ditch their drums, snag two of their fallen companions' guns, and charge up the hill, *somehow* dodging bullets and cannon blasts other soldiers fail to avoid.

Mental note: tell Mom Tommy and Hal are officially canceled.

Reenactments aren't playtime. We're trying to tell a story about things that actually happened. Even Noah rolls his eyes at me when Tommy and Hal suddenly decide to jellyfish to the ground without hitting a smoke pocket or reacting to a blast, gurgling and convulsing like they ran straight out of a swimming pool and into an electric fence.

Canceled.

Guys like them are the reason Mom doesn't let kids fight in the battle reenactments, even though hundreds of *actual* Union and Confederate soldiers really were just kids.

That's how I feel right now. Like a kid. Younger even—a little kid, anxious and confused and overwhelmed. Freaking Ben Oglevie's got me all messed up.

I try to focus on the pulsing in my forearms and the tightness growing in my biceps from the constant *ruh-ta-tuck-tuck* of my drumming. It only works for a few moments before my mind wanders again, until the smack of bodies against the fort doors brings me back to the battle. Enough Confederates, as planned, have made it up the hill, oh so carefully dodging enemy fire. A group of them hold a rough-cut log eight feet long and thick as a goalpost.

When it rams against the fort, it makes a thud to rival the cannon blasts. Behind the gate, unseen by visitors, our Union soldiers stand ready, counting the thuds before they wrench the wooden double doors open, shouting as if the ram broke through at last.

Now comes the fun part.

(Except I'm not having fun.)

Chase and I nod to each other and set our drums down beside Noah, who, as the least experienced drummer boy, has to stay behind to keep the rhythm going.

"Let's do this!" Chase yells, grabbing his rifle.

I pick up my own Springfield Model 1861 re-creation before I rush after him. Chase whoops loudly, but all the excitement I'd been feeling earlier is gone. This stupid rifle is more than four feet tall. I don't care if it was the most popular gun during the Civil War. It's awkward and heavy and hard to hold, especially now that my arms are sore from drumming.

By the time we make it to the ground, most of the Union soldiers are already through the gate and out on the field. Two men "died" just inside the fort and are sprawled out with their arms over their heads. Chase and I leap over them onto the flattened grass.

All up and down the hill, a few reenactors have given up shooting their guns and are brawling in rehearsed matches, swinging rifles and muskets like staves. It's all done as safely as possible, soldiers falling when the butt of a gun swings anywhere close to their head. All over, limp bodies pepper the grass, surrounded by all these faces watching happily from the sidelines as our battle reaches its climax.

When I was little, I sat with those families, wonder struck as the soldiers duked it out. The last few years, I've watched the battle from above as I drummed in the fort, the soldiers looking like video game characters. Now, with the battle inches in front of me, boots churning green to mud, the shock of metal meeting metal ringing in my ears, I feel like a dishrag wrung too tight. The idea of dying, even if it's all pretend, makes it hard to breathe.

I imagine Albert running beside me. Small as he is, his dark eyes are determined, his lips a flat, serious line. He doesn't whoop like Chase. He doesn't charge ahead with a fake gun and blanks.

For Albert, this was *real*. He spent three years in battle after battle, inches from death, watching his brothers fall, men and boys who didn't pop up grinning at the sound of applause.

Off to the side, the crowd cheers louder; and for the first time, all of this reenacting feels . . . *wrong*. This violence in front of me is nothing like the reenacting I do at the homestead or the schoolhouse. All those smiling faces, safe behind their ropes, make me want to hurl. Even if it is entertaining, war isn't *entertainment*—this is supposed to be a time to honor, remember, contend with one of the ugliest truths of America.

But people look happy.

I am the opposite of happy. Suddenly, the very last thing I want to do is keep running down the hill after Chase, who's waving and shouting, "Amos! Come on!"

Just as quickly, all my sadness turns into something else. Heat and rage.

Frustration.

I want to hit something.

Instinct takes over as the sounds of battle sweep over me. I race after Chase. We jog past arms and legs and chests, sidestepping gun butts.

But about halfway down the hill, I forget where I'm supposed to run. Even after all the practicing we did, my mind goes blank. I inhale. Hot air sears my throat. I don't see Chase anywhere. I scan the field, looking for someone to help.

Not far off, Darren is approaching a giant, ruddy, gray-bearded Confederate with shoulders that could get stuck in most doorways. Without thinking, I charge the pair, an animal cry spewing out.

Darren and Graybeard turn, confused by my appearance. I kneel, aim, and with a bear growl fire at the Confederate giant, who reacts a second too late with a groaning gut crumple. Darren gives me a nod and trudges deeper into the battle.

The crowd whoops and whistles. I shoot them a look.

This is not a game. This isn't a movie. It's not even theater. This is *history*. Real people died like this. People Albert *knew*. People Albert *loved*. They fought brother against brother, father against son, white slave owner against free Black man. Enslaved people fought their way to freedom, helping the Union army if they could, while others were forced to serve the Confederacy. It was brutal. I think about Jim at the homestead this morning, about all of the "simpler times" people. Nothing about war is simple. Nothing about *history* is simple. Not for people like me or Albert or Chloe or—

And something clicks into place. The past wasn't brutal for just *some* people. The 1800s weren't the good old days for *anyone*. Because when one person suffers, everyone suffers, even if they don't realize they are. Thoughts of Ben and his family take over my mind, all the hate eating up him and his family. But that's what hate does. It separates. It destroys. And that's what war is, isn't it? Hate in action. And hate doesn't care who you are. It'll hurt whoever it wants.

And here we are, rooting on hatred.

Cheering for anyone killing their family, their fellow Americans—it's all wrong. Wrong, wrong, wrong.

I reel back, staring at the man I just killed. He's some-one's son. He could be someone's father or grandfather. He could love someone. Someone could love him.

Something inside me tears that has never felt a crease or a bend or even a wrinkle.

My gun falls to the ground. Suddenly the sun is hotter than it was a second before. Much hotter. Dark spots crowd my vision and the world rocks under my feet.

Was my heart always racing this fast?

I collapse. The crowd cheers a few feet in front of me as I fall. Other soldiers run and tumble and fight around and beside me, but they're far away. Strangers in another dimension.

I blink and the world blurs out.

23

Tuesday, February 15, 2022

Dear Albert,

I'm sorry. I know it's been a while and that I should have written sooner, but, if I'm being honest, I wasn't going to write to you at all. Then Chloe got me thinking about you again. About all the LGBTQ+ people who still haven't had their stories told. And Ben. I think about Ben a lot. I worry about him. I miss him. It's not like we were anything more than friends, not *really*, but we were friends.

People shouldn't just vanish from your life.

Mom knows I've been low. She actually scheduled a meeting for me with the school counselor today, and it was the most uncomfortable thing ever.

Her: So, Amos, tell me about what's been going on.

Me: Nothing, really.

Me (translated): Nothing I want to tell *you* about. I just met you five seconds ago.

Her: Your mom is concerned about some recent

disappointments in your life. She said last month, the anniversary of your father's passing, hit you harder than it has in the last couple of years.

Me: I guess.

Me (translated): I guess Mom wants everyone to know my business now. I guess I don't have a say in who I share my problems with. I guess I'm not telling *Mom* anything anymore.

Her: Well, do you want to talk about it?

Me: Not really (plus, a shrug).

Me (translated): Not with you.

That's how our session went for almost an entire hour, Albert. I missed all of science and we were doing a lab, so now I have to make that up on my own time, which is so annoying. Ms. Counselor wanted to set up another meeting, and I didn't feel like I had much of a choice, so I'll be missing a class every Tuesday now.

I'm overjoyed.

Lies. All lies. I'm miserable.

And so is Chloe. When I told her our proposal wasn't even considered, she said, "You got to be kidding me. First the blacksmith apprenticeship, then Ben, and now our proposal? Watch. Next, they're going to tell us we can't even volunteer anymore. I'm too Black, and you're too gay."

She's right. It's like Chloe and I are only allowed to exist if someone in charge says it's okay. *This* is how stories of people with marginalized identities get silenced over and over again! And you know what I'm finally starting to figure out, Albert? It's not just our stories. What about other people of color? What about Native Americans? I don't even know how many people's stories aren't being told! It all makes me sick. I wish I could do more.

I wish Mom *would* do more.

As awesome as it was that she defended me to Mr. Oglevie, I don't understand why she didn't fight harder against Evil Santa or the LHP board and Mr. Simmons. I get that with the proposal, money was involved, but what Mr. Simmons did was WRONG, and if semi-bribing/blackmail isn't against the law, it should be. All of this makes me feel like I matter to Mom, but only when it's convenient for her. That my friends and I aren't worth fighting the real fights for.

So, the other night Mom had to get some prep done at the LHP and made me come with her, and I asked Chloe to come along. Figured it's better for us to be together when we're feeling low, and I'd rather not be alone with Mom right now.

We were wandering around the main gallery, playing a game we made up years ago. The gallery is full of sepia-toned and black-and-white photos from the 1800s. We take turns captioning the pictures to see who can make the other laugh harder.

Photo: A white man and woman, holding a baby, stand in front of a sod house. Neither of them is smiling.

My caption: A rare photograph of Midwestern hobbit pioneers. Going on this adventure was not their idea.

Chloe's caption: Hippies of the nineteenth century.

Photo: A group of white men with pitchforks stand around a wagon loaded up with hay. A white woman stands a little way off. None of them is smiling. (Albert, why was this no-smiling thing a trend?)

My caption: Haaayyyyyyyyy, gurl.

Chloe's caption: After hours of searching, they still hadn't found the needle.

Photo: A young white boy in a cowboy hat sits barefoot astride a calf.

My caption: It looked bigger in the catalog.

Chloe's caption: I've always wanted a pet boy.

At some point, though, we stopped laughing. We stood in front of a picture of a line of white women with identical haircuts and identical blouses hovering over identical sewing machines in a factory. Chloe said, "I should start replacing some of these pictures with ones I found of women blacksmiths. Not to mention a few more Black people." She paused. The gallery lights glowed amber on her skin. "I still think that's why Evil Santa wouldn't take me on. Because I'm a girl. And maybe because I'm Black, too."

My first instinct was to tell her that couldn't be it, that

Evil Santa couldn't be racist *and* sexist. But after an extra half second, I thought about all the history and racism I was only just now learning about. Of course, Brad could be acting racist and sexist.

"Maybe you're right," I said. "I think there's a whole bunch of bigotry we're fighting against. Racism, sexism, homophobia, transphobia. And it's all crap." My fingernails dug into my palms. "I keep wondering if Mr. Simmons had an ulterior motive for stopping our proposal, too, you know? Since they go to Holy Cross." I sighed. "Aren't we supposed to be past all this? Men against women, straight against gay, white against Black. I mean, we're all *supposed* to be 'equal' now. It's on paper—it's *legal*—but it obviously *isn't* equal, you know?"

"Um, *yeah*. I'm aware." Chloe gave me a very "duh" look. "You can't make people change just by *saying* things have changed."

"I guess . . . I guess I just thought the world was different now," I said. "But so much of it is still the same. It makes me so angry."

"Me, too." Her eyes wandered the walls. "Lots of things in *this place* make me angry."

I watched her gaze move from picture to picture. "What else?"

She gave me a funny look. "Can I show you something?"

I followed Chloe to a wall of photos from the Civil War, mostly boys and men from Illinois and Chickaree County.

She stood in front of one photo and said, "Tell me what you see."

Not sure what she was getting at, I said, "There's a soldier sitting in front of a tent with a little boy behind him."

"And what about the color of their skin?"

"The soldier's white, the boy's Black."

"Now read me the plaque describing the picture."

I did. "Shiloh, Tennessee: Unidentified Illinois soldier from the Twenty-Seventh Infantry holding a Springfield rifle."

Chloe's face fell a little. "Do you see it?"

I read it again, thinking I'd missed a typo or something, but when I looked back at the picture and really thought about what Chloe had asked me to do, it dawned on me.

"It doesn't say anything about the Black boy." I was ashamed I hadn't realized it right away. "Just the white soldier." There are dozens of other pictures on that wall. I wondered how many were like this. "What the heck?"

"I only realized it a couple of years ago," Chloe said. "I'd passed by this picture a million times, and I knew something about it bothered me, but I couldn't figure out what it was—and then it hit me. The Black boy has been totally erased. That description ignores that he's even in the picture, like he's as important as the tent or the sky. Just a part of the background. Even the freaking *rifle* gets a mention, but not him."

"That's messed up."

"I'm tired, Amos," Chloe said. "So freaking tired of fighting for people to be seen as people."

I couldn't stop staring at the picture or the plaque. Now that I saw it, I couldn't *not* see it, and it made me even angrier than I already was. "I can't believe I missed this all these years. I hate that I've been trained to see a white world." I turned to look at Chloe. I felt so bad that my best friend had been feeling this way for so long. That I hadn't been there for her. "We should do something. We should tell my mom about it."

"I already did." She picked at a fingernail. "She said 'she'd look into it.'"

The heat kicked on overhead. Warm air blew through the vent. "When was that?"

"At the start of last season."

That means for almost a YEAR Mom hadn't done anything to fix the plaque, Albert. A YEAR. I almost screamed. "I'm so sorry, Chloe. I'll talk to her."

"Things like this"—she pointed at the picture—"and our proposal and now the blacksmith apprenticeship . . . I feel like I'm always waiting for things to change, and I'm so sick of waiting." She looked at me. "I have an idea."

I followed Chloe out of the gallery. "Where are you going?" She kept walking toward the front desk, where Mrs. O'Grady welcomes visitors into the park. No one was there since it was after hours. Chloe reached around, pulled something out of the pencil holder, and nodded to me. "Let's go."

I followed her back to the gallery. She marched up to the plaque next to the picture of the white soldier and Black boy, uncapped the black Sharpie she'd taken from the desk, and in the neatest handwriting I've ever seen, wrote, "Also featured: unidentified enslaved Black boy in overalls."

"Oh my God. You did not just do that." I laughed.

Chloe capped the marker. "I just did."

"You are freaking awesome."

"I am kind of freaking awesome, aren't I?" She looked me straight in the eye. "Maybe, if we want things to change, we have to stop waiting. Maybe we just need to do something about it ourselves."

Chloe's right, Albert. It's time to stop waiting. Just because the exhibit proposal and Chloe's apprenticeship didn't work out, it doesn't mean our fight is over. We can tell Black stories. We can tell the stories of *all* people who have been erased from history. And we can still tell *your* story. We can find another way to get the word out about LGBTQ+ Americans from the nineteenth century. I don't need anyone's permission to tell the truth. If my mom and the board aren't going to listen to us, we'll do it on our own.

Albert, I'm going to find us a Sharpie, and then we're going to make sure the truth gets told in bold, black letters. I promise.

Your friend,
Amos Abernathy

24

★ ★ ★

Battlefield
Saturday, August 13, 2022—12:55 p.m.

The air is too thick in my lungs. Sunlight blasts my face. I'm soaked in sweat.

This must be what heat exhaustion and dehydration and worry all knotted together feels like. I close my eyes to block out the too-bright everything. Men are shouting everywhere. I'm pretty sure my heart has turned into a drum. *Rat-tat. Rat-tat-tat. Rat. Rat-tat.* I force my eyes open. Big mistake. The world is polka-dotted in black and gold. I'm pretty sure the ground is spinning. My eyes shut again.

It's only another ten minutes maybe, but it seems like hours before the battle ends and the audience is clapping. More noise, noise, noise. I roll onto my side. Oof—my stomach does not feel right.

The other fallen soldiers get up. They brush themselves off and bow stiffly to the onlookers.

I wait for the nausea to stop, but it keeps flattening me like a rolling pin. I don't move until something heavy kicks me in the foot. Shielding my face from the sun, I squint up. "What do you want? Can't you see I'm dead?"

Chase Pfeiffer holds out a hand. "Battle's over, nerd. Come on."

"I think I'm gonna die here a little longer."

"We have to get the field cleared," Chase says. "There's a game of cricket scheduled here in twenty minutes, remember?"

Something is always getting in the way of what I want.

Chase doesn't move, and I don't really want to catch a cricket ball in the face. Against my body's better judgment, I grab his hand.

When I come to standing, the field seesaws beneath me and my stomach lurches.

"Dude, you don't look so good."

And then there's vomit. So much vomit. All over Chase Pfeiffer's shoes.

"Dude!"

"Sorry." Another hurl. This time Chase steps back. I wipe my chin. My hands shake, but I feel a little better now. "Don't think I've had enough water today."

Chase drags his feet through the grass. "These are gonna reek. You owe me a new pair of shoes, dude."

I'm too shaky to even blush. "I am so sorry."

Someone off to the side calls my name. "Ew, Amos! Are you okay?" Cassidy is cringing behind the thin ropes, the rest of the Gay Cerberus behind her.

I wave them off. "It's fine. I'm fine!"

"Can we get you something?" Azul asks.

"No, that's okay. I'll meet you over at the main stage later."

Kevin squints at me. "You sure?"

"I'm fine, really!" I'm not fine. Really.

I'm freaking out about three o'clock, which *I cannot be sick for*, but I still feel like a human barf bag. The only person I want right now is Mom. Chase helps me find her at the Wakefield House, where she's supervising a group of junior volunteers. Most of them are playing with the skittles board. For half a second, I'm sure I see Ben standing next to it and my stomach does a double flip, but it's just some random guy. I tell my stomach to settle down.

No. More. Puking.

"Amos, are you okay?" Mom rushes to my side and sits me on the porch.

"Overheated, I think. Not enough to drink."

"He threw up on my shoes," Chase interjects.

"Oh, yeah. I owe him a new pair of shoes."

The back of her hand cools my forehead. "You're on fire. Let me get some ice—I'll be right back. Chase, you mind keeping an eye on the kids?"

"Sure thing, Miss A."

I tilt back until I'm resting against the wall. People pass by. Miserable as I am, I can't help but search the crowd for Ben's face. This *would* be the time he'd show up, when I'm most disgusting.

But there's no sign of Ben Oglevie.

While I chew the ice chips Mom brings back from one of the lemonade vendors, Noah Barringer comes running down the path.

"Heard you were sick," he says. "You left this in the fort." He hands me my haversack.

"You're losing everything today," Mom says. "Including your lunch."

"Actually, I didn't eat lunch." I'd been so busy thinking about Ben and Chloe and practicing with the guys before the battle, that I totally blanked on eating. Who does that?

Oh. I do. Real winner over here, folks!

Mom looks ready to smack me upside the head. "What do you mean you didn't have lunch? No wonder you got sick! Noah, do me a favor and run by the hot dog cart?" She hands him a ten. "A hot dog, a Gatorade, and some chips, please."

"Sure thing, Miss Abernathy." Noah runs off.

"Mom, I can get my own hot dog."

"I don't think so. You're going to sit right here and finish that ice *and* that hot dog *and* that Gatorade *and* those chips. You hear me? Last thing I need today is to call an ambulance for my own son." She scrutinizes my face. "And, um, did you find him yet?"

"You can say his name."

"Ben. Did you find *Ben* yet?"

"Nope." I sigh. "Ben got Chloe involved, so there's this weird game of telephone going on. But I told her to tell him that if he wants to talk to me, he needs to do it himself."

"So she knew he was coming?"

"Not until this morning, I guess."

"Huh. That's very un-Chloe-like, to keep things from you." She touches my forehead again. "A little cooler. Good." She hesitates. "Do you know *when* you're going to talk to him?"

"No clue. Everything seems to be on his terms."

"Isn't it always?"

Uh-oh. Mama Bear's back.

Noah Barringer returns with a hot dog, potato chips, and a bottle of blue Gatorade. "Hope you don't mind mustard on your hot dog."

"Thank you." Mom unwraps the hot dog and shoves it in my hand. "Now go on ahead to your next station, Noah."

Despite the queasiness and bitter aftertaste of bile in the back of my throat, I devour the food. Mom tells me to slow down or I'll get sick again, but I can't stop. It doesn't just taste good—it *feels* good to eat. My whole body's waking back up.

"Guess I really was hungry." I take another sip of Gatorade.

"You're too old not to be taking care of yourself, Amos. Don't do that to me again." She runs her fingers through my sweaty hair. "Where are you supposed to be right now?"

"Printshop, I think, but I need to find Chloe first. I want to know if she talked to Ben yet. Whatever's going on with him, I just want it over with."

"Finish that Gatorade and I'll let you leave. And don't take too long with Chloe either—Deborah isn't gonna be happy you're late. She already gave me an earful this morning. Come get me if you start feeling sick again, okay?"

"I'm fine, Mom. Don't worry."

"I'm your mother. It's my job to worry."

I hate when she says stuff like that. Like mothering is an occupation she's fed up with.

I down the last of the blue drink, hold the empty bottle out for her approval, and then make my way toward Chloe.

25

Sunday, March 13, 2022

Dear Albert,

So, remember that time Chloe was a total boss with that Sharpie? Turns out that was only like boss level one. Chloe has officially reached boss level one million.

Okay, let me back up.

The first weekend of March is always the start of the spring season at the Living History Park, and OH. MY. DRAMA.

Chloe and I were on our way to our new apprenticeship assignments—me at the printshop with Deborah Weaver, and Chloe at the stables with Sandy McGinnis—when we noticed Chase Pfeiffer tying on an apron at the blacksmith shop.

I swear, actual lightning crackled in Chloe's eyes.

"You have got to be kidding me," she said.

That's right, Albert, after Brad Pinot said he wasn't taking on *any* apprentices, apparently he accepted one "last-minute emergency" request at the end of February. (The reasons I'm upset with Mom keep piling up.) Who does he suddenly find acceptable to work in the shop? Chase Pfeiffer, who, don't get me wrong, is a great guy—but he's a straight, white, cisgender boy.

Brad almost dropped a red-hot horseshoe when he saw Chloe. "Uh, hey, kids."

"You told me you weren't taking on any apprentices this year."

"It's within my rights to change my mind," said Brad. "I was really doing Amos's mother a favor. Otherwise, Chase here wouldn't have had an apprenticeship."

Chase flushed.

"I thought you were apprenticing in the stables?" I asked him, genuinely confused.

He sniffed. "Allergies."

Chloe stepped up to Brad. "So, you're telling me you could make an exception for the allergic white boy, but you couldn't figure it out for a Black girl who is—no offense, Chase—*way* more capable, passionate, and knowledgeable about blacksmithing?"

"Hard not to take offense," Chase mumbled.

I shook my head at him to back down.

"Listen, Chloe, the hard truth is that Chase is simply more suited for the position." Brad hung his tongs on the wall. "I'm sorry."

"You think he's stronger than me? Or is this because he fits your historical expectations of what a blacksmith's apprentice should look like?"

Brad paled. "What? No, this has nothing to do with that."

"But you see how it looks, right?" Chloe whirled to me. "Don't you, Amos?"

"I do."

Chloe leaned around Brad. "What about you, Chase?"

His eyes bounced from me to Brad to Chloe. "I, uh, yeah, guess you're kinda right. . . ."

Brad sputtered. "I—I honestly can't believe you think I'm some sexist, racist jerk. This wasn't an easy decision."

"I'm sure it wasn't," Chloe said, "but that doesn't mean you made the right one."

Brad started to say something and then stopped. There was long, super uncomfortable pause. Then he scratched his scruff, told Chase not to touch anything, and walked out of the shop.

Now Chloe and I were both pretty fired up. At the end of our shift, we booked it straight to Mom. We found her in her office. Judging by the tense look on her face, I think she was expecting us.

"You made Brad agree to make Chase his apprentice but not Chloe?"

"I know how it looks," Mom said, "but I was in a tight spot."

Chloe kept her tone eerily calm. "Ms. Abernathy, you know I love you, but this is jacked. I mean no disrespect when I say this, but I can prove I'm a better fit for the blacksmith shop than Chase."

Mom rubbed her temples. "The decision's been made. I'm sorry. I'm just glad everyone *has* an apprenticeship."

"I thought Brad wasn't taking any apprentices. How much of a fight did Brad put up when you asked him to work with Chase?" I asked.

"Amos, not everything is a fight," Mom said. "He understood the situation. Plain and simple."

"Don't you think that's a little fishy, though?" Chloe said. "Me? No way. Chase? No problem."

"When Brad's made up his mind, there's not much I can do to change it. And some battles just aren't worth fighting when there is a simple solution."

Chloe mumbled, "Me not being in the blacksmith shop is not a solution."

I couldn't believe Mom honestly said that. "You're telling us that it's not worth it to stand up for my *best friend*?"

A vein in Mom's neck bulged. "That's not at *all* what I meant, and you know it, Amos."

I wasn't giving up. "But aren't you, like, Brad's boss? Why are you letting him tell you what he will or won't do?"

Mom stumbled over her words. "I'm not— Brad— No one is telling me what to do, Amos. Chloe, I'm sorry, but some things in life just aren't fair. Now I need to finish up so we can get out of here. I'm starving."

Chloe and I went from fired up to molten, but there was no more talking to Mom. She straight up ADMITTED that this was *her* decision. I couldn't believe she didn't see how unbelievably unfair and *complicit* she was being in this weird racist/sexist power struggle. The whole situation was so OBVIOUSLY wrong. I thought my mom was better than that.

I was so ticked. Chloe was supposed to come over for dinner, but I didn't want to be around Mom. Chloe didn't either. So she okayed it with her parents, and instead of going to my house, Mom let me have dinner with the Thompsons.

When we got to Chloe's house, Mr. and Mrs. Thompson were just sitting down to eat.

"Hey, kids," said Mr. Thompson cheerily. His skin is dark copper, and he's got a couple of freckles under his left eye that look like a constellation. Fit as he is, he has a big belly like Darren, which makes me wonder if that's something all men eventually grow into. "Come sit down. We just finished fixing tacos. Grab a plate."

Mrs. Thompson passed us the package of flour tortillas. She was in one of her "comfy shirts" which is just one of Mr. Thompson's old T-shirts. Her short bob framed her face in rich brown coils with reddish highlights. Chloe's mom has one of the truest smiles I've ever seen on a person—she's always *actually* happy to see you. "How're things at the LHP?"

Chloe and I just looked at each other. Then Mr. and Mrs. Thompson gave each other a look like "uh-oh."

"What happened?" asked Mr. Thompson.

While we ate, Chloe and I told them about seeing Chase at the blacksmith shop and talking to Brad and arguing with Mom. They listened patiently, but Mr. Thompson kept shaking his head and Mrs. Thompson seemed to take a bite each time she wanted to jump in.

When we finished, Mr. Thompson reached out and held Chloe's hand. "I'm so sorry that happened to you, Chloe. My gut says I ought to give Han"—his eyes flicked to me and my cheeks instantly went red—"er, this Brad a piece of my mind, and I just might, but I want to know what *you* want?"

I know he wanted to say he had words for Mom, too. I guess he didn't want to mention that with me sitting there, but I kind of wish he had.

Chloe pulled her curly hair around her neck so it all lay on her left shoulder. "I don't want you to get involved, but I also don't know what else to do. I already tried talking to Amos's mom."

Albert, when she said that I got even more embarrassed and angry. Mom failed her, which felt like *I'd* failed her.

Mrs. Thompson pushed her plate forward like she'd lost her appetite. "Amos, I'm sorry if this offends you, but

Chloe, I think it's time we go *above* Hannah. If you want, your father and I will call—"

"No," Chloe said. "I want to take care of this."

Mr. Thompson nodded. "Then how about we help you write an email to the board?"

So that's what happened. The next day, Chloe and her parents drafted an email to the park board. She sent it to me to look over.

Dear LHP Board,

My name is Chloe Thompson. I've been a volunteer at the Chickaree County Living History Park for four years, and I love spending my time there.

This past fall I applied to be an apprentice at the blacksmith shop and was denied because the lead interpreter was not taking on apprentices. But when the season started yesterday, I learned that Brad Pinot has agreed to let a white boy apprentice for him. To be clear, I am a Black girl.

This discrimination is unacceptable. I hope that you will look into this situation and work with Ms. Hannah Abernathy to correct this injustice. My parents and I look forward to hearing how you have addressed this situation.

Sincerely,

Chloe Thompson

I felt a little guilty about going behind Mom's back, but *three* times now Chloe had tried to get Mom's help and *three* times Mom let her down. It was freaking unacceptable. And now that I could see what was really going on, each one of those failures felt like a slap in my own face. I couldn't not do anything.

But Mom stepped into my room before I could send a message back to Chloe.

"Hey," she said. "Can I talk to you?"

I didn't say anything, but she kept talking anyway. The shadows under her eyes were darker than usual. "I can't stop thinking about what you and Chloe said in my office yesterday. About what's worth fighting for. About fairness. And—and I realized I messed up."

Now I was listening. "Ummmm, *yeah.*"

She cleared her throat. "I really need to talk to the two of you." She sat down on my bed with a heavy sigh. "Can you call Chloe?"

I called her right away and put her on speaker.

"Hi, Chloe," Mom said. "I've been thinking a lot about what you and Amos said last night, and how I reacted hasn't sat well with me. I hate that I told you this wasn't a battle worth fighting. I was wrong." Mom took a deep breath. "I was going back through email threads, trying to better understand my thinking and why I allowed Chase to apprentice but not you, and I then came across an email from you that I'd completely forgotten about.

"I'm not sure if you remember, but a little more than a year ago you emailed me about a picture of a Black boy in the gallery, about how he isn't listed in the photo description. I told you I'd look into it, and then I never did. And I then never got back to you. I couldn't believe I'd dropped the ball. That I hadn't made your request—your very *important* request—a priority. I felt terrible—I *feel* terrible. I want you to know that the picture of that boy is on the top of my list for tomorrow."

Mom paused and stared at the phone. Chloe was quiet at first, but then she said, "Okay."

From the sound of her voice, I could tell she wasn't impressed with Mom. I didn't blame her. Mom was *so* late figuring all this out.

But Mom went on. "Looking at how that happened, that revealed some ugly things in me I didn't want to look at. When it comes to race, and, hard as it is for me to believe as a woman, *gender,* I have been irresponsible. I've been telling myself we don't have issues at the LHP. It's uncomfortable for me to admit, but I'm starting to see just how much racism and sexism are embedded in how we operate. And now that I see it, I will not stand for. If Chase can be Brad's apprentice, so should you."

I held my breath. Chloe was quiet on the other end of the line. And then she said, "Are you for real?"

Mom laughed nervously, but she looked a little more relieved. "I called Brad a little bit ago, and we've both come to the conclusion that we were wrong. *Very* wrong. Chloe, I am so, so sorry that I didn't listen to you *multiple* times. That I didn't stand up for you the way I should have. I *do* value you and your passion and all of the time you've given to the park. Moving forward, I'm putting policies in writing that explicitly protect and address diversity, equity, and inclusion at the LHP. I've gone along with the 'this how we've always done things' attitude since I took over, and I'm done with that. I'm going to set things right, beginning with you. If you still want to, starting next Saturday, both you and Chase will apprentice with Brad."

Chloe shouted, "*Yes.* I do, very much."

"I hoped so," said Mom. She had tears in her eyes. "I'm learning a lot from you and Amos. I want to thank you both. And apologize for not being there for you sooner. I'm so sorry, Chloe. I hope that you can forgive me."

"Thanks," said Chloe. "I really appreciate that, Ms. A."

"I can't wait to see you in action." Mom smiled for the first time since she came into my room. "Are your parents around? I'd like to speak with them if they have a minute. I owe them an apology, too."

Don't get me wrong. I am SUPER happy for Chloe, but I can't help but wonder where this version of Mom was a couple of months ago. If she can fight for Chloe, then why not me? *I'm* her son. Doesn't she think fighting LGBTQ+ discrimination is just as important as fighting sexism and racism? What about ME?

Oof. Gross.

I just reread what I wrote. This is embarrassing. Chloe gets a giant win, and I am making it all about *me*. Talk about a cisgender white boy moment. This isn't about me. I didn't have to fight to get my apprenticeship because of my race or my gender. It's okay to celebrate Chloe's win without using it for my own battles. UGH. I should know better. I *do* know better.

God, Albert, I have so much freaking work to do. Some-day, I hope, I won't have to remind myself that I am NOT the center of the universe.

OKAY. Enough of ME, ME, ME. After our chat with Mom, Chloe and I decided not to send the email to the board. (Honestly, I was kind of relieved we didn't have to. But you know I would have!)

Then yesterday, Brad surprised all of us. Not only did he seem moderately okay to have Chloe starting as his appren-tice, but he *also* apologized. Then Chloe got right to work next to Chase. I haven't seen her that happy (or fierce) in a while. She looks good with a hammer. And she is officially the FIRST Black woman blacksmith EVER at the LHP.

She's not just living history—she's *making* history.

So, there might be some hope left for humanity after all.

In other news, yesterday was also the grand opening of the updated exhibit. *Shoes of the Nineteenth Century.* Chloe and I made sure to ~~judge it~~ *experience* it first thing.

The exhibit is a single, rectangular room off the main gallery in the visitors' center. The Simmonses used their footwear connections to find a whole bunch of boots and clogs and pattens from the 1800s. The shoes sit in glass cases like priceless jewels.

It's literally the weirdest, most boring thing I've ever seen.

Actually, it gets weirder. At the front of the exhibit, the Simmonses commissioned an oversized re-creation of the shoes Abraham Lincoln supposedly wore while in office. It's super hokey, but visitors have been taking a million pictures and posting to social media. (I hate to admit it, but it's been a nice boost for the LHP.)

At the end of our ~~judgment~~ experience, I told Chloe, "I still can't believe this is what the board went with. Even the Chickaree County Women's Society's 'infamous quilts' idea was better than this."

Chloe lowered her voice. "Want me to get a Sharpie?"

I laughed. "Not yet."

That's all for now, Albert. (Aren't you impressed that I made it through a letter without mentioning Ben?)

Oops. I guess I mentioned Ben. FREAKING BEN OGLEVIE.

Yeah, I still miss him.
Your friend,
Amos Abernathy

26

★ ★ ★

Blacksmith Shop
Saturday, August 13, 2022—1:33 p.m.

The smell of woodsmoke pours out of the blacksmith shop. I cough. I will never understand what Chloe likes about this job.

"You all right?" she asks from behind the anvil. Sweat drips down the sides of her face, but she looks right at home with a hammer in her gloved hand.

"This heat is awful," I say. "How can you stand being in here more than thirty seconds with the furnace blazing like that?"

"I was a volcano in a past life."

Brad Pinot walks in with two bottles of water and hands one to Chloe. "Here to see my star pupil?"

In the months since the Controversy of the Blacksmith Apprenticeships, Brad Pinot has changed a lot. He went from adamant that Chloe would be in the way, or at the very best a struggle, to taking serious pride in her work.

I'm not surprised at all how quickly she turned him. There were a few burned forearms and smashed fingers at first, but Chloe picked up the basics within the first two weeks. By the third week, she was wielding tools like a blacksmith pro. Every safety measure Brad lays out, she follows with precision.

Chase Pfeiffer, however, turned out to be clumsy with a hammer, and within two weeks of starting the apprenticeship asked to be transferred to the homestead.

Brad did not object.

"With the arms on that boy, I figured he'd be a natural," Brad said. "Goes to show I don't always know what I'm talking about. Never too old to learn you're wrong."

Chloe has become something of a celebrity as the first female blacksmith at the Chickaree County Living History Park. The *Chickaree County Herald* even ran a feature on her with the headline "Forged in Fire: First Female Blacksmith Ignites Historical Intrigue." More girls than ever have been interested in visiting the blacksmith shop. She even got asked for her autograph. But I think what made Chloe most happy was that Mr. and Mrs. Thompson made a big deal about it. They even framed the article and hung it on the wall next to Cadence's awards.

I get out of the way as a group of teenagers I don't recognize enter the shop, ogling the furnace. "Can I talk to Chloe for a minute?" I ask Brad.

He sets down his water bottle. "Be quick. We have another demonstration in two minutes and folks aren't coming to see me anymore."

"I'll be right back," Chloe says, resting the hammer on the anvil with a grin.

It's heaven stepping out of that nasty heat. I take a massive gulp of water before saying, "Did you see Ben yet? I don't want to get ambushed."

Chloe sucks her lips into her mouth. "Yeah, I saw him. I told him to talk to you."

"What did he say?"

She looks irritated. "Weren't you the one who said you want this to be between the two of you?"

"Yeah, but I still want to know if he said something."

"He didn't say much," says Chloe. "Just, like, 'okay.'"

"'Okay'?"

"Yup."

I squint at her. "He didn't say anything else? Just that one word? *Okay*?"

"He said he'll find you later."

"Later *when*?"

Chloe shrugs. "I don't know! Amos, I'm tired of being in the middle of you two. You'll see him when you see him."

"Sheesh. Fine."

A familiar voice turns both our heads.

"Hi, honey!" says Mrs. Thompson. She and Mr. Thompson

wave as they near us. They're both wearing LHP T-shirts and sipping lemonade.

Chloe hugs her parents, but I'm so anxious about Ben and the performance that words come out of my mouth before I can think. "What are you doing here?" I ask instead of saying hello like a normal human.

Mr. Thompson wraps his arm around Chloe and pulls her tight to his side. She gives me a "duh" look while he says, "We're here to see our number one blacksmith!"

"Oh, ha ha, right." I scratch the side of my head to hide how ridiculous I feel.

Fortunately, Brad's head pokes out of the blacksmith shop at just the right moment. He waves at the Thompsons, taps his watchless wrist at Chloe, and disappears.

"I've gotta go," she says looking directly at me. "I'll see you soon, okay?"

I can tell that what she really means is "Everything will be all right." I nod. "Okay."

Mr. and Mrs. Thompson follow Chloe into the shop. Mr. Thompson turns back and waves, saying, "I guess we'll see you at three, right? Chloe said there's a thing or something?"

That catches me off guard. I didn't know her parents were coming! But I say, "Right, yeah. Three o'clock. See ya there!"

Then I book it to the printshop.

27

★ ★ ★

Sunday, March 27, 2022

Dear Albert,

In movies, when a character wants to show another character they care, they make a grand, sweeping gesture—blast a favorite song from a boom box outside their window, send a hundred bouquets, show up looking gorgeous in an unexpected place—and it works. Both characters get emotional and sappy and they live happily ever after.

I'm not sure why it's taking me so long to figure this out, but real life isn't anything like a movie.

A week ago, I decided I needed to see Ben and that I was going to make it happen and nothing was getting in my way. Since he hadn't responded to emails, texts, phone calls, or handwritten letters, my options were reduced to one thing: showing up in person.

Obviously, I was terrified of seeing his parents, his dad in particular, who I'm pretty sure scarred me for life with that phone call (not an exaggeration), but I kept thinking about Ben having to live with him and how unfair that is. I figured that if Ben has to endure that discomfort on a daily basis, I could handle a few moments of suffering. It would be worth it if I could hear Ben tell me that his parents lied, that he did miss me. And if it was true that Ben didn't want to see me anymore, well, I deserved to hear it straight from him.

So yesterday morning I got on my bike and rode the two miles to Ben Oglevie's house. It was sunny and a little chilly. One of those days that can't decide if it's winter or spring. The whole trip there I thought about turning around, but my feet kept spinning the pedals and before I knew it, I was standing on his doorstep with my helmet under my arm and my backpack strapped tight to my shoulders.

Nathan, the brother who picked him up from the movie theater, answered the door. It was better than facing Mr. Oglevie, but seeing him still made my stomach squirm. It took him a second to recognize me.

"What are you doing here?" he said.

"I need to talk to Ben."

Nathan pulled the door closer to him, as if that would muffle the sound of us talking. "I don't think that's such a good idea. Things have been—"

"I'll be quick. Please."

He peeked over his shoulder and then turned back to me. "Don't move."

The door shut. I waited two minutes, which doesn't

sound like a long time, but when you're standing at the front door of the house that belongs to people who don't like you, trying to talk to a friend you once had a crush on (and maybe still do?), two minutes feels like two days. I almost chickened out, but then the door opened a wedge. Ben slid through the slight gap and closed it quietly behind him.

Seeing him, being near him again, all of the old feelings came rushing back. My heart sped up, my stomach dropped, I got too hot and chilled all at the same time. I couldn't stop staring.

He's changed since last November. His hair is longer, swooping low just above his eyebrows. He's gotten taller, a little more muscly, almost overgrown and too tight inside his own skin. But his brown eyes are the same. For a moment, it was like we traveled back six months in time.

Then he said, "What are you doing here?"

I couldn't help my eyes darting to the curtained windows, wondering how close his family was, if prying eyes were watching us, waiting to see what the queer kid would do.

"I . . . I miss you." It sounded so stupid when I said it, but it was the truth.

He scratched the back of his neck. "Amos, you need to go."

He wasn't getting rid of me that easily. "I've tried to get ahold of you."

"I know. You need to stop."

"Are your parents still upset about what happened?"

Ben's eyes twisted to the house. "Amos, I— My dad— what he said to you . . ."

"It's not your fault."

I've never seen his eyes turn so dark, almost black. "I know it's not my fault."

"I didn't come here to fight."

He snorted. "Then why did you come here?"

A car passed behind us. Across the street, a dog barked after it. His owner hollered through a window for him to quiet down. This was so not the Ben I remembered. The edge in his voice, the flatness of his face. Maybe he really didn't want anything to do with me.

But I wasn't giving up. "I brought you something," I said.

His eyes narrowed as I slung the backpack around my body. From the front pouch I pulled out a gallon ziplock bag.

"Are those skittles?" The tiniest hint of a smile sneaked through his tense expression. At least, I want to believe it did.

"Painted them myself," I said as he opened the bag. "They're all our favorite Marvel characters."

He pulled out two of the wooden pins. "I don't recognize these guys."

I blushed. "Those are, uh, us."

I was sort of embarrassed he couldn't tell right away. I

painted us in our LHP costumes, me in my blue shirt and him in his gray. I even took extra time to mix brown, black, and white to get the perfect shade for his eyes. His fingers wrapped tightly around them. Then he put the skittles versions of us back in the bag and resealed it.

"I thought maybe you could come up with a new set of rules for a superhero version of the game." I paused. "And that maybe we could hang out sometime?"

He fidgeted with the edges of the plastic bag. "Amos . . ."

"Just as friends," I said, maybe too fast.

He kicked at the cement stoop with his foot.

The front door opened behind him. His mom appeared. "Ben, what are you . . ." Her voice trailed off when she saw me. She looked almost panicked, but a polite smile lifted her lips. "Amos. I didn't know you were here."

"Hi, Mrs. Oglevie."

"He was just leaving, Mom."

She perked right up at that. "Well, hurry up, Ben. Dad's almost got breakfast on the table." She looked at me. "Good-bye, Amos." She closed the door, but I had this feeling she hadn't gone far.

Ben backed up against the door. "I've got to go."

"But maybe we could still hang out sometime?" I said.

The curtain ruffled. I think Ben saw it, too. "Amos, I *can't.*"

"At least think about it? Please."

I wish I'd kept my mouth shut, because Ben Oglevie exploded. "What don't you get, Amos? I don't want to see you. I don't want to be your friend. I was confused. I—I never *liked* you. It was all a mistake. Just leave me alone!"

He shoved the skittles I'd painted for him at me. He rushed back inside, and the door slammed shut. Voices murmured, but they faded quickly, and I was alone on the stoop holding those stupid skittles.

My hands shook. My eyes stung.

Albert, I sobbed like a freaking baby. Right there. On his porch. And on the whole ride home. When I got back, I chucked my helmet at the garage door. The hard plastic shell cracked right down the middle, but I didn't care. I don't care. There's no point.

I was wrong, Albert. So wrong. There's no fixing what happened between us. There's no going back to the way things were. There's no saving Ben.

Amos

28

Printshop
Saturday, August 13, 2022—1:40 p.m.

None of this makes any sense. Why wouldn't Ben just tell Chloe when he wants to talk to me? Since he more or less handed me our friendship in a million pieces (well, nine pieces) the last time I saw him, you'd think he could at least give me *that*. I mean, what the heck does he even *want*? What could he possibly have to say to me that he hasn't already made crystal clear?

I'm not wanted. I get it.

Like a dummy, I'm letting myself think for half a second that maybe, just *maybe* I didn't totally suck at reaching out to him. That Ben's here to tell me he still cares. That he wants to be friends. That his parents changed their nineteenth-century ways and now their house is one giant rainbow glitter fest and—

Oh my God, Amos. Stop.

What is wrong with me? It's like I *want* to keep getting hurt.

As I pry open the screen door of the printshop, I shove Ben to the back of my mind. Come on, Amos, you're a printshop apprentice now, not a heartbroken loser. That version of you will only get in the way of reciting facts about newspapers, chases, and that ginormous printing press that fills half the room.

"You're late."

Deborah Weaver, the head printshop interpreter, is white, in her late fifties with snowy, shoulder-length hair and pruned lips. Since she's a freelance reporter for the *Chickaree County Herald*, you'd think the printshop would be a happy home away from home for her, but she's always complaining. Mom constantly tells me she can't wait until I'm old enough to take over the exhibit (highly confidential information, of course).

"Sorry," I mutter, throwing an apron over my head. "Has it been busy today?"

Deborah fans herself with a stack of inked pamphlets from the mini handpress. "More people coming in today than I've seen in weeks. I forget how Civil War Remembrance Week brings out every man, woman, and child within twenty miles of Chickaree County. Every year I tell myself, 'Deb, it'll be manageable. You've got this.' Then I get here and all I want is my lawn chair and a bottomless mimosa. But I know this place couldn't run without me." She sighs heavily. "Remind me to tell your mother about my thoughts for parking next year—folks have been complaining all day about finding spots."

I sort through the small metal letters pulled from the upper and lower cases—large wooden boxes with tiny compartments for each character. The upper case holds capital letters; and the lower case, as you might expect, holds lowercase letters, plus italics and punctuation. It's kind of fun when people realize how the phrases "upper case" and "lower case" came to be.

"I'm sure Mom will be thrilled to hear your plans," I lie.

"And don't even get me started on the battle reenactment," she goes on. "You know not a soul came in here while that was going on? And yet all us volunteers up and down the street were expected to stay at our posts. Next year we should close up all the buildings during the battle. Some of us wouldn't mind seeing it every once in a while, you know."

Breathe, Amos. *Breathe.* Do not freak on Deb because you're ticked at Ben.

"Why are all these letters out of the case?" I ask.

I really shouldn't be surprised that this question only gets her more worked up. "Your mom promised this group of Girl Scouts they could have a special printing of

216

a message they designed. Lord almighty! They got about halfway through filling the chase and decided it was too much work. Kids these days want everything in an instant! No patience for anything worth the time. Of course, they didn't bother to put anything back and I haven't been able to. The arthritis in my hands has been acting up again." She fans herself with the pamphlets. "At least you finally made it. I need a break."

Oh, thank God.

"That's fine," I say. "I'll get these sorted for you. Take your time."

On her way out, Deb says, "Ah, I almost forgot." She pats down the apron she just hung up. Out of the front pocket, she produces a folded-up piece of paper. "Some kid dropped this off a little bit ago. Said to give it to you."

I have now lost control of my mouth. "You've got to be kidding me."

"Excuse me?"

"I meant, who's it from?" I ask, even though I know.

"Don't remember his name, but he looked familiar. Kind of tall and scrawny, blond. Soft voice."

I unfold the note without looking at it. "Was it Ben Oglevie? He volunteered here last year."

She nods slowly. "You know, I think that was him. Really shot up over the past year. Hardly recognized him."

Ben Oglevie! I'm so sick of these freaking notes. Why

217

can't he face me on his own? Just talk to me or leave me alone!

"All right," Deb says. "I'll be back in a few." The spring-loaded door slams behind her.

I smooth the paper flat using the corner of the wood counter.

> *Dear Amos,*
> *Please don't be mad at Chloe. I'll meet you at the*
> *main stage at 2:45.*
> *Ben*

The wall clock tick, tick, ticks in my ear. Ben has got to know that's the worst possible time to talk. Just minutes before I go onstage and do the riskiest thing I've ever done in my life. He wants me to have a complete and total break-down!

And yet, the list of things Ben might say plays over in my mind:

I'm sorry for what I said.

I'm sorry my parents are the worst.

I'm sorry I didn't try harder to be your friend.

The door creaks. I snap upright. A trio of elderly white people scoots through the entrance, and my interpreter mask settles over my face.

"Welcome to the Chickaree County Printshop. Here

we print a daily newspaper on a steam-powered printing press—" My eyes drift to the clock. It's already 2:15. Half an hour before I have to face Ben.

Half an hour to decide what to do.

One of the old men coughs. "I was a paperboy back in the day. Sold 'em a dime apiece. How much these go for back in—when you from again?"

"Our shop was built in 1861, the first year of the Civil War," I say. "Our papers cost ten cents at the time."

The old man chuckles. "Ha! I sold papers almost a hundred years later and they cost the same." He turns to the curly-haired woman next to him. "Jane, how much we pay for the *Herald* yesterday?"

"Oh, I think I paid almost two dollars for it, Bill." The woman has a soft, round voice.

Bill chuckles again. "A hundred years and no change. Then, not even a hundred years more and it goes up by nineteen hundred percent! Too much change, Jane. Too much." He smacks his lips, eyes roving dreamily over the printshop. "Times were good back then. Life was so simple. Didn't cost so much just to get by. Things made more sense."

It takes everything in me not to challenge him. Albert, Walt Whitman, Abraham Lincoln, the Black boy in that photo in the gallery—they all fight in my mind to be the first to prove Bill wrong. Love, friendship, freedom—none of it "made more sense" back then. Maybe for Bill, a straight,

219

cisgender white man, things would have been simpler, easier, cheaper, but not for the rest of us.

The world needed that nineteen hundred percent change. And it still isn't enough.

But I smile, swallow all my feelings, and continue the tour of the printshop, silently counting down the seconds to 2:45.

29

Thursday, April 21, 2022

Dear Albert,

You know who I shouldn't be thinking about anymore? Ben Oglevie. But here I am, going back over all the notes we took for our proposal, thinking about the best way to get our research out into the world, and I'm thinking about Ben. You know who I blame for making me think about him?

Abraham *freaking* Lincoln.

Because I guess I ENJOY FEELING AWFUL, I kept going with Ben's research of our sixteenth president. I *thought* I knew a lot about Lincoln. He was always my guy, my go-to historical figure, but I learned a whole bunch of shady things about him this week and now I'm frustrated and confused. Did you know the Emancipation Proclamation didn't really free everyone who'd been enslaved? Or how about the fact that Lincoln didn't even think Black people should have the same rights as white people? WHAT THE HECK? How is one of my historical heroes also a villain?!

But it's not *all* bad, Albert.

So, remember that time Ben told me he "wasn't exactly straight"? Remember that poem he showed me that Abraham Lincoln wrote? Well, not only was Lincoln kind of definitely racist, he was also very likely not completely straight.

Sorry, Mary Todd.

Apparently, like, when Lincoln was twenty-eight, he had this best friend, Joshua Speed, and the two of them lived together in Springfield and shared the same bed. Not super scandalous or anything, but record has it they were "inseparable." What's even more interesting is that when Joshua's father died and he had to move back to Kentucky, Lincoln decided to go with him. Not super weird either, but then I found out Lincoln BROKE OFF HIS ENGAGE-MENT with Mary Todd to chase after Joshua. I KNOW, RIGHT?! At some point Joshua married a woman (dang heteronormativity), and we all know good old Abe married Mary Todd, but they didn't have the best relationship (maybe because he was definitely sort of totally actually possibly gay???).

~~Good Lord, I hope that never happens to Ben.~~

NO MORE BEN.

From what I've been reading here, there's no solid evidence that Abraham and Joshua were "in love" with each other, but choosing a friend over a fiancée . . . I mean, that sounds like a whole lot more than friendship to me.

And that's not the only time Lincoln had a close "friend-ship" with a man. After he married Mary Todd and became president, he had this bodyguard named David Derickson, who was pretty good-looking, and they got . . . really close. Whenever Mary Todd was out of town, David slept with the president. He even wore Abe's nightshirts.

Albert, I'm pretty sure the president of the United States of America doesn't *have* to share his bed with anyone if he doesn't want to, even back then, so this was a *choice*. Abraham and David *wanted* to sleep together. Of course, there's no evidence that anything happened, but there *are* records of people saying how unusual it was for Lincoln to bring Derickson into his bedroom.

Could you imagine? What if Abraham Lincoln, one of the most influential men in the history of our country, was actually gay or bi? Even just the possibility makes me feel . . . seen. Like I have this deeper connection with the past than I did before. But then I remember he was a secret-not-so-secret racist and I realize that being marginalized doesn't automatically make you an ally of people from other marginalized identities. You can be gay *and* racist. Part of me is, like, *duh*, and another part is just sad. We should all be helping each other.

~~I wonder if Ben is sad.~~ NO.

The hardest part is that this is all a lot of guesswork.

I can't go back and ask Lincoln or Speed or Derickson what was really going on in their heads (or in their beds), so we can't say for certain which team they were on. That's personal business, anyway. But I do feel one step closer to proving to the world that not *everyone* from the nineteenth century was straighter than a ruler.

The other thing I keep thinking about is how sad Lincoln and Speed and Derickson must have been. If they really did love each other, if they really did want to be together and society told them they couldn't, it must have broken their hearts. I don't know how Lincoln did everything he did— having a family, running a country, starting and ending a war—*and* battled the feelings he might have had.

If he *was* gay or bi or not exactly straight, I bet it was like he had his own civil war going on inside him. Wanting to be himself, or having to be what everyone expected of him.

Living back then as a queer person would have been the worst. I'm lucky to be alive now. Lucky I have people who love and accept me exactly as I am.

Not like Ben.

Now I really can't stop thinking about him. How he might be the biggest liar I ever met, how he played me for months and led me on and then totally disappeared. How he crushed me.

Or how his parents are totally homophobic, how we can't even be *friends* because of those same nineteenth-century expectations. How, maybe, just *maybe*, that boy still really likes my face.

There's a civil war still going on, Albert, but it looks different today. Actually, I think there's lots of civil wars happening all around us, all over our country—inside people's minds and hearts, between parents and kids, between brothers and sisters.

There's even a civil war inside me.

Maybe I'm being stupid, but if Ben *is* fighting right now, I want to fight with him. I want to fight *for* him. I'm just not sure what to do. I can't talk to him, but I don't want us to get trapped like Abraham and Joshua and David. We have the chance to be different. To live a different life. Even if we're only ever just friends, I want Ben back—if he wants me back. We need each other.

I just don't know how to get him to believe that.

Your friend,

Amos Abernathy

30

★ ★ ★

Printshop
Saturday, August 13, 2022—2:20 p.m.

My blood pulses in time with the almost silent *click-click-click* of the printshop clock. It's been quiet, so I've been trying to go over my notes for three o'clock, but my thoughts are all over the place.

Ben. Albert. Ben. Mom. Ben. Chloe. Ben—

The chime rings. The door opens. In walks Meredith Simmons.

I do not have time for this girl. "What are you doing here?"

She slides her finger along the counter like she's inspecting for dust. "The heat is simply oppressive, Amos. A sojourn in your presence seemed quite necessary." Her finger and thumb rub together daintily. "Though the upkeep of your little establishment leaves a girl wanting."

"Meredith, I am so not in the mood." I leave the counter and take a seat on a stool by the printing press.

"Oh?" She bats her overly mascaraed eyelashes. "Well, I thought you might be interested to know that I spotted some of your, shall we say, *perverted* acquaintances gathering down by the main stage. I thought that was odd. You never know what sexual deviants might be up to. So, I moseyed over for a spell, and you know what? I learned some very interesting things."

I'm no longer sitting. *Perverted. Sexual deviants.* I assume she's talking about my GSA friends.

"You're lucky there's a counter between us, Meredith."

"Don't be silly." She laughs. "Even a prissy boy like you knows better than to hit a girl. Besides, don't you want to know what I learned?"

"Not really."

Her elbows rest on the counter and she props her head in her hands. Ringlets of hair bounce as she shakes her head, "Then you won't mind if I share what I've discovered with your mother? Or my father? About the little charade you and your freaks are about to force upon the tender ears of Chickaree County at three o'clock?"

You have got to be kidding me.

I walk slowly to the counter. "Meredith, you can't say anything."

She pouts. "What's to keep an honest girl like me from spilling all that sweet tea?"

My world is on fire. If Mom or Mr. Simmons finds out

now, they'll shut us down before we even have a chance. With all the calm I can muster, I say, "Please, Meredith. If there is even one sixteenth of an ounce of good in you, you won't say anything. *Please.*"

"Oh, Amos," she says. "My unending goodness is precisely why I must share what I know. It's only right!" She wears the cruelest feline grin.

This doesn't just push me over the edge. It's more like I leap off the edge and transform into a fire-breathing dragon. *"What is your deal? Why are you always trying to hurt me? It's like you're obsessed with me!"*

Her smile falters. She steps back. "Amos, I assure you I—"

"Just stop, Meredith!" I simmer. "Tell me. Why is it always me? Why can't you just leave me alone?"

Her hands drop to her sides. Her plasticky smile cracks, and she stumbles over her words. "It's not— Amos, I don't— I'm not obsessed!"

And the most absurd realization hits me. Maybe it wasn't actually *Sarah* who had a crush on me back in fourth grade. "But . . . you are. Did you—" I laugh. "Do you have a crush on me?"

"What? No!" Her cheeks bloom bright red. "That's disgusting."

Oh my God. That's *it.* Meredith Simmons *like*-likes me. I can't believe I didn't see it before. What even is my life?

228

Now I'm smiling like a cat who caught a mouse. I finally have the upper hand. "Sorry, Meredith. You're just not my type."

"I do not have a crush on you!"

"Whatever you say."

She growls. "I'm telling your mom! Right now! You can't stop me."

Before I can figure out how to do just that, she slaps the door open and marches out, and in walks Deborah Weaver.

"What's riding up her knickers?" she says, handing me an enormous plastic cup of lemonade. "Your mom says you got sick earlier and you need to stay hydrated. Don't know why we can't have this godforsaken festival in a cooler month!"

"Thanks, Deb." Meredith, Ben, Mom, Mr. Simmons, Deborah, this lemonade—there are too many things going on at once. I've got to get out of here.

"Do you think I can leave a little early?"

Deb wags her finger at the giant lemonade. "Not until that's good and gone. Don't need you passing out on my watch. You just keep tidying up!"

"Deb, I'm fine. I swear. But I need to go."

She plants her hands on her waist. "Amos Abernathy, do not make me call your mama!"

I stick the straw in my mouth.

Exactly two minutes and seventeen seconds later, I rattle

the remaining ice in the cup and leap over the counter. "Done."

"Where do you think you're going?" Deborah asks. "You've still got fifteen minutes on your shift."

"Sorry, Deb," I shout over my shoulder. "I've got a battle to prep for."

"Battle?" she shouts after me. "What are you talking about? Don't tell me there's another one!"

Oh, just you wait, Deb. The biggest battle's about to begin.

31

Thursday, April 28, 2022

Dear Albert,

They say there are stages of grief. I can't tell you what all of them are, but the two I've felt over the past couple of weeks are heartbreak and fury. Not sure how many more I have to go through before this awfulness is over.

I've tried everything to stop thinking about Ben, but he's stuck in my brain-teeth like an annoying piece of spinach. All I want is to floss him out of my life, but nothing's working.

Last week I moped around so much Mom eventually wore me down and I finally told her what happened that day that I rode my bike to see Ben. I thought she was going to be mad, but she wasn't.

She pulled me into a hug and said, "It'll be all right."

"You don't get it." I hugged my knees to my chin, toes curling over the edge of the chair. My eyes burned. I pinched the top of my nose. "We're supposed to be living in this *progressive* time, but people are still treated like garbage and discriminated against all the time. It's like no matter how much we do, it'll never be enough. There's always more fighting to be done. Just one time, I don't want to have to fight."

Mom inhaled through her nose, taking a seat at our kitchen table. "Amos, you take on too much. You don't have to fight every battle that comes your way. Just because you're out and proud, it doesn't mean you have to be out and proud for *everyone*."

"But if I don't fight, who's gonna do it?" I traced a dark grain in the table with my finger.

"Weren't you just saying you didn't want to fight? That's a bit of a contradiction."

My feet slid off the chair to the floor. "That's *exactly* what's happening. Everything is pulling me in opposite directions. Fight or don't fight. Ben or no Ben. Do what's right or give up. I'm at war with myself and I hate it." I wiped the pre-cry blur from my vision. "I'm just tired of it, Mom."

She scooted closer in her chair and took my hand. "You're thirteen. You're too young to be tired."

I shrugged. "Well, that's how I feel."

She nodded slowly. "These past few months haven't been easy on you. The exhibit proposal; my mess up with Chloe's apprenticeship; everything with Ben; and, even though you won't talk to me about it, I *know* that having Darren around has been a big change."

Her words were like onions. Two roly-poly tears streaked down my cheeks. She didn't make a thing of it, which I liked.

When I didn't say anything, she went on. "You can talk to me, Amos. Is there something else bothering you?"

I shook my head. There weren't enough words to describe what was going on inside me. It was Ben and it wasn't. Same for Darren, and for the exhibit proposal. It was everything and nothing. I was this busted helicopter spiraling out of the sky, but it wasn't the machine that was broken—the problem was the pilot's hands were tied together and all he could do was watch as the whole hunk of metal crashed into the sea.

Crashing. That's what I was doing. Not because *I* was broken, but because I'd lost control. Maybe I never even had control in the first place. But I couldn't put that into words just then. All I could do was shake my head. I wasn't sobbing hysterically or anything. Everything was just . . . draining out of me. Someone had turned the faucet to full blast and broken off the knobs.

Somewhere between all the tears I asked, "Why didn't you fight harder for our proposal? Albert needed you. *I* needed you. You fought for Chloe. Why not me? The board would have listened to you eventually."

Her shoulders sagged. "I did, Amos. I tried. Really. But some minds are too stuck. Too unwilling to see beyond the edges of the box they were told to live in."

"So, you just gave up?" I said. "Raised the white flag. Game over. *Finito*?"

Mom's jaw clenched. A vein pulsed in her forehead. "Not game over. More like halftime. A retreat to regroup and reassess. There will be other opportunities. You'll see."

I wiped my eyes dry. "What if there *aren't* other opportunities? What if I missed my shot?"

"I'm sure there will be. Just give it time."

Albert, I think Mom's trying. Really. But at the end of the day, I still don't think she completely gets what I'm going through. She doesn't understand what it's like to be gay. So, I asked Ms. Wiseman if she could stick around after our GSA meeting today.

I plopped into a desk in the third row. Ms. Wiseman gave the whiteboard a final swipe, set the eraser on the ledge, and then perched on a desk in the front row, feet propped up on a chair. She gave me this look, eyes squinted, lips smooshed.

"Why are you looking at me like that?"

She cocked her head. "I had this feeling you were going to come talk to me."

"That's weird. How'd you know I wanted to talk to you?"

She tapped her temple and grinned. "Teacher's intuition.

234

Plus, I'm a little clairvoyant. Long history of witches in the family."

Ms. Wiseman knows how to be funny and serious all at the same time. It's one of the things I like most about her.

I smirked. "I always thought you liked Halloween a little too much."

"Hey! I was being serious." She snagged a crumpled piece of paper and tossed it at my head. "Enough about me. What's going on with you?"

I fidgeted with the pocket of my hoodie. "You remember me talking about Ben, right?"

So, I reopened THAT continuously scabbing wound and told her about everything that had happened: his brother seeing us at the movie theater, his parents finding out, all the way through to Ben telling me he never really liked me. By the time I was done talking, Ms. Wiseman was slumped into the desk chair, sitting in it backward, facing me, her chin cradled in her hands. Her cheeks were red, and I wasn't sure if she was going to start crying or throw a stapler across the room.

"I'm so sorry that happened to you, Amos," she said.

"It's just so unfair."

"As long as there are people on the planet, life will be unfair, but that doesn't mean we have to put up with hatred or bigotry. What his father said to you, how Ben treated you—that was wrong."

The next thing I said didn't come out easily.

"I'm afraid I messed him up." It felt even worse to admit than I thought it would, but it all just kept spilling out. "That it's my fault. That I got in his head, or I pushed him to be something he's not. That I got him in trouble for sort of kissing him." I paused. "Is it weird that I'm talking to you about this?"

"Only if you think it's weird."

The word vomit continued. "I mean, how do you ask someone out on a sort of date and then *never talk to them again*?"

"Sounds like it's more complicated than that."

I sighed. "I just want to know the truth. If he really never liked me, or if his parents are just forcing him to say that."

Ms. Wiseman exhaled slowly. "Amos, we both know coming out isn't an easy process. For some people, families make it even harder. Whatever the truth is, give Ben time. Maybe that's what he really needs."

Albert, I'm so sick of people telling me to wait.

Your friend,

Amos Abernathy

32

Main Stage
Saturday, August 13, 2022—2:36 p.m.

I wipe the perspiration off my forehead with my sleeve. As I near the fenced-off grassy area in front of the main stage, I tilt my head at the volunteer stationed at the entrance gate. She waves and I keep walking.

The massive structure is the only thing in the whole Living History Park that doesn't fit the nineteenth-century vibe. A canopy of metal beams arches over a raised black platform. Can lights shine down on big-box speakers, instruments, and snaking cables from local bands. Most of the music isn't even close to historically accurate, but outdoor concerts are a major draw, which means more money for the LHP. I'm fine with anything that might mean we aren't so dependent on the Simmonses for funding.

I wonder if Meredith found Mom yet.

No. It doesn't matter now. No matter what Meredith or

Mom or Mr. Simmons or anyone might do, this is happening. But first things first: find Ben.

I half expect to find him on the stage, waving me down, but the only people up there are members of a local bluegrass band, shifting equipment around. I scan the crowd. There are dozens of families, couples, and groups of friends. People in lawn chairs. People on blankets. The smell of funnel cakes and sunscreen and hot dog water is everywhere. More sweat dampens my forehead. Still no Ben. A hokey banjo recording twangs out of the speakers. A group of young kids dances in circles near the front of the stage. No Ben.

No Ben. No Ben. No Ben.

Hesitantly, I trudge around the back of the stage to the white tent where the on deck acts prep before going on.

That's where I find Ms. Wiseman and her girlfriend—I've never met her before, but I recognize her from the photo in Ms. Wiseman's classroom—and Chloe. The Gay Cerberus is there, too, along with four more of the GSA kids. They shout and wave when they see me. And not far off, Jessica strums a guitar, while Trish and few other people from Grace Hill sing along.

"Oh, good," Ms. Wiseman says. "I'm glad you got here a few minutes early. Amos, this is my girlfriend, Nadia."

Nadia takes my hand. She's got warm, brown skin and looks like she might be of Middle Eastern descent. She's a little taller than Ms. Wiseman, too. The hem of her long calico dress sweeps the tops of her shoes. Her nose ring twinkles in the afternoon sun. "Amos! I have heard so much about you!"

"Yeah. You, too."

"Are you doing all right, Amos?" Ms. Wiseman says.

"I'm fine, but, uh, have you seen—"

Ben, Ben, Ben.

Chloe's hand is on my shoulder.

"Don't shoot the messenger, but he's in there." She points to the tent.

"Ben?"

Her eyebrow goes up. "No, the Easter Bunny."

"Very funny."

She leans her head in close to mine. "Look, I know you. I'm sure you've got a million thoughts rolling around up there." She knocks my skull with her knuckles. "Remember whatever he has to say, you are one heck of a human being and no one is good enough for my best friend. You hear me?"

"Thanks." I hug her. "Hey, um, I'm sorry for what I said earlier."

"I'll forgive you if I have to."

I hug her harder. "You know I love you, right?"

"You better." She laughs, hugging me back. "Love you, too."

Ms. Wiseman clicks her pocket watch. "We've only got twenty or so minutes before we go on, Amos. I know you probably have a lot to say, but—"

"Don't worry. I'll keep it short."

I look back at Chloe one more time before lifting the tent flap.

"You got this," she says, two thumbs-up. So cheesy.

Bright spots cloud my vision as the flap falls behind me. My eyes adjust to the dim light. A throat clears. Light motes take the shape of a boy sitting in a folding chair.

Ben.

Even sitting he's taller than I remember. His cheekbones are more pronounced. Waves of blond hair fall a little farther down his forehead. Beneath his Avengers T-shirt, he is, um, kind of *buff*, as if his muscles were working overtime since we were last together. He stands up. "Hey."

I freeze. Somehow, he's familiar and new all at the same time.

How he can be all "what's up?" after everything that's happened?

"Hi." My voice is smaller, quieter than I mean it to be. I don't want him to think I'm weak, like I'm going to fall apart seeing him again. I clear my throat. "So . . ."

Our words overlap:

"Amos, I, um—"

"What are you doing here?"

Ben releases a half-hearted laugh. "Um, well. Where do I even start?"

I don't laugh with him. "How about the beginning?"

Ben nods somberly. "Why don't you take a seat?" He points to another folding chair with a black suit draped over it. "I know we don't have long."

"Yeah, you really have a way with timing."

"I know, I know. Just sit, please?"

I do and cross my legs. "Well?"

Ben sits across from me and leans in, palms pressed together, knees bowed out. There's a long pause, but I don't let myself say anything.

He sighs heavily. "Amos, I'm so sorry. I am so sorry for what my dad said to you. I'm sorry I didn't stand up for you. I'm sorry I made you think I didn't care."

My arms fold in front of me. "You just expect me to forgive you?"

"I know, I get it, but it's complicated. Things are so different for you. I can't— Amos, you barely even had to come out to your mom. But just me questioning, even *thinking* I might like you, felt . . . dangerous. I had my whole family, my whole church, my whole *life* telling me it's wrong for me to feel that way. They said I needed help. They said I just needed to 'pray harder.' You have no idea what it's like living in a house with that hovering over you all the time."

The hurt in his voice almost breaks me. Now I really

can't look at him. "You're right. I don't know what that's like. I'm sorry. I just . . . Losing you hurt so much."

"It hurt me, too, even if I didn't show it," he says. "But after you, uh, after the, um . . . movie theater"—I think we're both blushing, but I still won't look at him to check for sure—"things got real messy. Church folks talk, and I guess someone from Grace Hill was talking to someone from Holy Cross about our exhibit proposal and they made their way to Mom and Dad. I got an earful for helping you, but I swore that's all it was. Helping a friend. But then Nathan saw you, um, sort of kiss me. He told my parents, they lost their minds, and you know the rest. It was awful. Worse than awful, Amos."

My insides crumble. I owe him the truth. "Ben, it's my fault that your parents found out about the proposal. I was talking about it at church one Sunday and I, uh, accidently said you were helping. I totally wasn't thinking. I—I'm so sorry. I didn't mean to make things worse for you. And the kiss . . ."

He starts to speak, stops, and starts again. "Amos, it's okay."

"But it's *so* not okay." That old urge to wrap him in a hug comes back. (*Stop it, Amos!*) "I didn't know it was so bad."

Ben shrugs. "How could you?"

My eyes narrow. "So, what changed? Why're you here? *How* are you here?"

"A whole heck of a lot's changed," Ben says, leaning back in the chair. "These past few months have been absolutely insane. You remember me talking about Danny, my oldest brother? Well, turns out Danny is actually super gay."

My jaw falls. "Excuse me?"

A small, satisfied smirk crinkles Ben's cheek. (*Ugh*, he *is* still cute.) "I know, right? He moved away more than a year ago, after he graduated college, and we hadn't heard much from him. Danny was always a bad communicator, so we chalked it up to him not checking his phone and Danny being Danny. But the truth was, he had a boyfriend, and none of us knew it.

"My brother Nathan texted him at the end of April to let him know what was going on with me and how Mom and Dad freaked out, and the next thing I know, Danny is on our doorstep. Mom and Dad were excited to see him until he mentioned Lars and—"

"Lars?" I can't help but raise an eyebrow.

"Yeah, *Lars*. He's very Swedish." Ben grins. "Anyway, instead of getting angry, Mom and Dad got all mopey and down, calling themselves 'failures,' as if they'd raised two homicidal maniacs instead of two gay sons. Danny wasn't having that. He called them out and, honestly, it was the best thing in the world. Mom and Dad listened and fought and listened and finally we all came to a sort of agreement."

Information overload is hitting me hard. I can't process

243

this fast enough. There's no way this is real. "So, what? They're suddenly cool with gay people?"

"Um, not exactly," Ben says. "But the needle's moved from 'You're Going to Hell' to 'We're Learning to Practice Tolerance.'"

"Ugh, *tolerance*. I hate that word. I *tolerate* body odor, not human life."

Ben's hands fly up. "I know, but baby steps, okay? This is huge for my parents, Amos. Like, *really* huge."

Even though I want to shout "This isn't about your parents! This is about *you*!" I stay cool and say, "Yeah, no, I know. I just—I want more for you."

A soft smile spreads over Ben's mouth. "I know."

Those lips.

Stop, Amos.

Feedback from a speaker screeches onstage. The sound reminds me that it's almost time to go on, but I don't want to leave now.

"If all of that happened months ago, why did you wait so long to come see me?"

"Figured you hated me. But then I got your text last night."

I shrug. "You could have just texted me back."

"No, I had to see you. After everything that happened, I didn't want this to be a text or even a phone call." Ben picks something off the ground that looks like a . . . dead animal?

244

He stands. "Nathan drove me here, but then I freaked when I walked in. That's why I went to find Chloe first. She told me to talk to you, but I couldn't do it, so I wrote that stupid note. I—I always make things more complicated than they need to be."

"True." I smile.

"Hey! I'm trying here."

"Keep trying."

"Anyway, what I wanted to tell you is that I'm ready. For everything."

My fingers and toes tingle. "What does that mean?"

"Well," he says, "for one, I'm ready to say—" He laughs. "Funny, now that I'm actually going to say it, I can't." He exhales and shakes out his arms. "I'm gay. *Ha!* I did it."

I am crying on the inside, but like a dork I say, "Nice to meet you, Gay. I'm Amos."

He laughs and smacks my arm. "You are such a nerd." He holds up the dead animal, and I realize what it is: a fake beard. "I'm also ready to get this show on the road."

"Wait. Are you serious?" I laugh.

"Indeed I am. Chloe got me up to speed."

I can't help it. I hug him.

He hugs me back.

33

Friday, May 6, 2022

Dear Albert,

The Sharpie has arrived.

I repeat: the Sharpie has arrived.

Here's what happened. Chloe and I were eating lunch in Ms. Wiseman's room, which we've been doing since Meredith Simmons has made the cafeteria even more of a nightmare than it usually is. (Whoever thought "Super Sloppy Joe Monday" was a good idea needs to seriously reassess their life choices.) But back to MEREDITH, the Apple Grove Middle School Sloppy Joe's only competition for Most Likely to Make You Vomit. Every day she walks by our table to brag about how great the shoe exhibit is and how hard she worked on it and how the president of the United States wants to shake her hand (okay, I made that last part up). The point is, I've just about had it with her! Ms. Wiseman's room is the only safe place where we don't have to hear Meredith's voice for forty-two glorious minutes.

Most of the time Chloe and I talk, and Ms. Wiseman grades or plans or does some online shopping, but sometimes she listens in. Occasionally, she'll say something back.

Today I was pretty ticked off because this redheaded white kid in Language Arts, Blaise Freeman, was trying to argue that we shouldn't have to read a poem by Langston Hughes because his family doesn't agree with Hughes's "lifestyle." My jaw dropped. Langston Hughes was not only gay, but *Black*. I don't think Blaise realized just how insanely offensive he was being.

Obviously, this piqued Ms. Wiseman's interest. "What did your teacher say to that?"

"She said he needed to 'separate the art from the artist.'"

Ms. Wiseman covered her cringe too late. "I see."

"But Butthead Blaise didn't let it go," Chloe said. "You know what he did?"

Ms. Wiseman tensed up. "No?"

"Closed his book and slid it across the desk," she huffed. "Claimed he didn't have to read something that went against his beliefs."

"Then what happened?"

Chloe and I exchanged a look, and I said, "Our teacher told him he could read an alternative poem."

I've never seen someone's lips disappear so far into their mouth. Ms. Wiseman capped her pen and set aside her grading. "And that was it? That's how she left it?"

Chloe's eyes rolled. "Yeah, that's how *she* left it."

"What does that mean?"

I chopped a carrot in half with my front teeth. "I had other plans."

Chloe wagged a cheese stick at me. "*This* kid stands up in the middle of class like he's Buzz Lightyear of Star Command and says, 'So what, Blaise, are you done talking to me?' Every head in the room whipped around. Mrs. Williams choked on her coffee. It was awesome."

"You didn't," Ms. Wiseman gasped. "Did you really?"

I nodded. "Blaise didn't know what to say. He fumbled and eventually said, 'It's different with you,' and so I asked why it was different, and he said, 'Because you're Amos. I *know* you.'"

"As if his prejudice doesn't transfer from dead poets to living classmates," Chloe muttered.

"Mrs. Williams kept telling us to quiet down. That we are all entitled to our opinions, but I couldn't take it anymore," I said. "I'm so tired of straight, white, cisgender people getting their way, while the rest of us have to be quiet so all of them can feel comfortable. If Blaise wanted to ignore one queer Black voice, I wanted him to see who else he'd have to erase."

"So, Amos asked Mrs. Williams if he could stand at the front of the room, and she was like 'What?' but by then there was no stopping Amos," said Chloe.

"What did you do?" Ms. Wiseman looked mildly horrified.

"Sheesh! Don't look at me like that. All I did was talk."

None of these things will make any sense to you, Albert, but in class I listed off:

The Lord of the Rings movies

X-Men movies

Avengers: Endgame

The Big Bang Theory

BD Wong

Billy Porter

Janelle Monáe

Panic! at the Disco

Lil Nas X

Elliot Page

Demi Lovato

"After I was done, I looked at Blaise and said, 'If you're going to erase Langston Hughes, a famous, respected poet, who else are you going to cut out of your life? All of these movies, TV shows, and singers are queer or have a queer performer. You were Gandalf for Halloween two years ago. I know you listen to Panic! at the Disco, and *Endgame* is your favorite movie. When you deny one of us, you deny all of us. You don't get to pick and choose. You're not erasing homosexuality, Blaise; you're erasing human beings.' Then I sat down."

"Mic drop," said Chloe, making an explosion sound.

"Do I want to know what happened next?" Ms. Wiseman asked.

"A couple of kids clapped, and I got a lunch detention tomorrow for disrupting class, but Blaise didn't say anything else. He even read the poem when Mrs. Williams started teaching again."

"Wow."

"Yeah, I know," I said. "And I thought it was over, but then Blaise caught up to me after class and said, 'Hey, I didn't mean to offend you,' and I told him he did, and then he said, 'Sorry. Honestly, I forgot about you'—which I also tried not to be offended by—'It's different when you actually know someone who's, you know, like *you*. You're cool. I don't want anything bad between us. We good?' I told him we were, and we did that weird high-five-handshake-hug guys do when they're trying to be sincere. And that was it. Over. Done. But I can't stop thinking about it. What happened with Blaise happens with so many people. Queer people aren't weird aliens. We're just like everyone else."

"From your lips to God's ears," Ms. Wiseman said.

"But it got me thinking," I went on. "About the Forgotten Voices exhibit. How maybe that wouldn't have done any good for someone like Blaise—it would have been pictures and words, but nothing *human*. It wouldn't have put a face to the problem." I paused for dramatic effect. "I can't believe I didn't think about this before. We're historical reenactors at a *living history park*. We literally bring history to life."

"Well," Chloe said, "not *literally*."

Ms. Wiseman smirked.

"You know what I mean. My point is, we need an opportunity to get in front of people. Like a rally or something. We can actually *show* them we exist. Blaise didn't even think about me until I pointed it out, and we've been going to school together for years! I bet lots of people are like that."

Ms. Wiseman adjusted her glasses. "We're not supposed to pick favorites, but I just can't help it with you two."

Chloe and I grinned at each other. There's something ridiculously satisfying about teachers breaking rules, even if it's the most ridiculous rule in the book. I mean, *obviously* Chloe and I would be her favorites. Duh.

Ms. Wiseman spun her chair to face her computer. "You know what? I think . . . I've got just the right opportunity for you."

She flipped her screen to us.

"Why's my mom emailing you?" I asked.

"She's wondering if I want any time on the main stage opening day of Civil War Remembrance Week, since I'm double-dipping between school district and LHP responsibilities. I was going to talk to Mr. Bader about putting a choral group together to perform a selection of music from the era . . . but I'd rather give the spot to you. Fifteen minutes in front of all of Chickaree County, if you want it."

"Are you serious?"

"I am."

I bear-hugged Ms. Wiseman right in her rolly chair. We both almost fell over. She laughed and hugged me back with T. rex wrists since I'd trapped her arms.

It wasn't until we were walking to next period that I realized what I needed to do.

"There's no way Mom can know," I told Chloe. "Not until it's already happening. I don't want her trying to stop the performance."

"You really think she would?"

I looked at her like "Where have you been?" and said, "The board might not like our plan, and if Mr. Simmons or Meredith get wind of it, you know there'll be trouble. I don't want Mom to have to choose between me and her job."

"Maybe she'll be able to convince them this time."

"I'm not willing to risk it." Mom's proved over and over that she'll side with the board, and this performance *has* to happen.

"So, you're going to lie to her?"

I swallowed. "She's just going to find out the truth a little late is all."

Part of me feels guilty for keeping this from Mom, but, Albert, I'm so excited. I've got big plans—bigger than just me. I already talked to Azul from the GSA about helping out. They were super stoked.

We've got another shot, Albert, and this time, we're not losing.

Your friend,

Amos Abernathy

34

Main Stage
Saturday, August 13, 2022—3:00 p.m.

Heat ricochets off the black stage into my face. My forehead is so sweaty I could put out a fire just by turning to look at it. I'm still wearing my Union blues from the battle reenactment. Good lord, it's warm. A shudder runs through my bones as I survey the field, the eyes of hundreds of families, many I've known my whole life, staring up at me. Some look wiped out by the heat. Others bored. And a few look downright unpleasant. But a handful are watchful, waiting. I wonder how they'll look by the time we're through.

That's if Meredith doesn't show up with an army of people trying to stop me.

Ms. Wiseman reaches for the microphone. "Good afternoon, everyone! How y'all doing today? Having a good time kicking off Civil War Remembrance Week?"

The most pathetic holler rises up from the crowd. Oof. Goodbye, last of my morale!

"I *said*, ARE YOU ALL HAVING A GOOD TIME?" A giant smile colors her voice, and even my nerves can't stop the urge to grin.

A few faces brighten. I spot Mr. and Mrs. Thompson sitting in their blue bag chairs off to the right. They put their hands next to their mouths and whoop, and this time the crowd happily hollers with them. In the far back there's even a "yes, ma'am!"

My jitters suddenly aren't so bad. My grin's almost a smile now.

"Much better," Ms. Wiseman says. "Now that I have your attention, my name is Emily Wiseman, and I'm a teacher here in Chickaree County"—someone shouts her name with a whoop, and she waves them off, smiling—"and I was going to give you all a local history lesson, but one of my students—one of the most remarkable young men I know—has organized something I'd rather you hear instead. Here's what I ask, folks: listen with an open mind and heart, and listen close. Think you can do that for me?"

Finally, some enthusiasm.

"They're all yours, Amos." Ms. Wiseman gives my shoulder a squeeze and takes her place.

Now there's electricity crawling up the back of my legs and cotton balls sticking to my tongue. Cool, cool, cool.

Someone sticks their fingers in their mouth and whistles. Maybe she's gotten them *too* excited.

255

Just breathe, Amos. I glance back to make sure everyone's ready. Jessica and Trish have their guitars strapped over their shoulders, amped up and ready to go. The Gay Cerberus and the rest of the GSA are spread out across the stage, staggered into two rows. Ms. Wiseman; her girlfriend, Nadia; Chloe; and Ben stand just behind me. Each one of them looks perfect in their period costumes. Even Azul with their blue hair.

Okay, *maybe* we kind of look like a pioneer show choir featuring the Union Army, but—

Ben catches my eye. Half a heartbeat vanishes into thin air. He mouths, "You've got this."

I nod and turn back to the mic.

That is one overripe crop of stares. Oh boy.

Albert, please be with me now.

I take off my soldier boy cap and grin nervously at the crowd. "Thanks, Ms.—" Feedback crackles. *So cringy.* I step a little farther from the speaker and the noise fades. "Ha, sorry 'bout that. Thanks, Ms. Wiseman. Hi, everyone. My name's Amos Abernathy, I'm thirteen, and I've been a historical reenactor here nearly my entire life."

That gets me a few smiles. The Living History Park *is* Chickaree County's claim to fame. People take pride in that.

The more I look around, the less the crowd looks like a mob. I see the Dennis family who used to live down the street from us. There's Mr. and Mrs. Romano who run the diner on Seventh. Even Pastor Shirt made it out. I bet Jessica told him. What's weird, though, is that he's standing next to Gareth Gunner, the pastor from Holy Cross. He's wearing a red tank top and is so sunburned that he looks like a human fire hydrant. His expression is sour, and I haven't even started yet. I figured there'd be some homophobic people in the crowd, but I didn't plan for an outright bigot.

I glance back at the main gate. (*Phew*. Still no Meredith.) "There's something else you need to know about me," I go on. "I'm gay. I've known for as long as I can remember. Last year, a friend of mine got me thinking about the past, about LGBTQ+ folks who lived in an era I spend ninety percent of my life thinking about, and I realized I didn't know hardly *anything* about *anyone* from the queer community who lived in the 1800s, especially not from around here."

And there go the smiles. Flatlined. *Beeeeeeeeep.*

Okay, not everyone. A few smiles. I can work with a few smiles.

Then one family, smack-dab in the center of the field, starts packing up their cooler and folding their blankets. Pastor Shirt gives me an encouraging nod, but Gareth Gunner has gone pale. His arms are locked across his chest. I swallow. Somewhere, though, someone whoops encouragingly. I think.

I almost start up again but notice a flash of movement at

the entrance gate. Meredith, leading her father by the hand, Mom and Darren just a step behind.

My voice cracks. "One of the first people I found when I googled 'queer people of the nineteenth century in Illinois' was Albert D. J. Cashier, who lived practically next door to us. Learning about him changed everything. Originally, I hoped our opportunity to update one of our museum exhibits meant we might be able to feature queer American history of the nineteenth century, but that didn't work out."

Mom is just staring at me. No expression. *Gah.* I wish she was frowning or *something.* At least I'd know what she was thinking.

"So my friends and I, we put together a little performance for you, celebrating the lives of LGBTQ+ Americans from the nineteenth century. For the next few minutes, I'm going to become Private Albert D. J. Cashier, of Company G, Ninety-Fifth Illinois Regiment."

I fix my cap on my head and plant my feet firmly in place, so I don't shake right off the stage. Then I take a deep breath and speak in a slightly Southern, slightly Irish accent. "Good afternoon, ladies and gentlemen. My name's Albert D. J. Cashier, but that wasn't my name when I was born in Clogherhead, County Louth, Ireland, on Christmas Day, 1843—you see, my folks believed I was a girl, so they named me something else, but it never fit.

"When I was eighteen, I donned men's clothes and

boarded a ship bound for America. The Civil War was just beginning, and after I settled in Belvidere, Illinois, I knew I had to fight—all men worth anything did. I enlisted and served three long years. I may have been the shortest man in my company, but I got along well with just about everyone. Over many months, I fought nearly forty battles. In Vicksburg I was just about captured by a Confederate, but I muscled his gun away and made my way back to safety.

"After the war, stories of women who'd dressed as men to fight came out. Many of them went back to living in dresses and sewing and bearing children, but that wasn't me. I was Albert through and through."

Mom hasn't budged, but Mr. Simmons is jabbering in her ear. All around, people are whispering to each other. Gareth Gunner's checking his watch.

I go on, "I made Saunemin, Illinois, my home, working odd jobs here and there. Everyone knew me and loved me as Albert, because that's all I ever was to them. No one knew I'd been anything other than Albert until I was run down by an automobile. I was sixty-seven then. Fractured my leg bad. It was the doctor who fixed me up that discovered I wasn't quite like other men he knew."

Gareth Gunner leans into Pastor Shirt's ear. Pastor Shirt shakes his head sort of irritated, but I can't tell if it's at me or Gareth Gunner.

"But the doctor kept my secret," I say. "You see, I wasn't

posing as anything. I wasn't trying to cheat a system—I *was* a man, but sometimes it's hard to convince people of that, even if you assure them you're a 'he' and a 'sir.'"

A little bit of gravel rolls around in my stomach. Darren wedges himself between Mom and Mr. Simmons, trying to get him to walk away. Mom's still just watching me.

"When my mind started to go a few years later—dementia—I was moved to a state hospital, where they were not so kind to me as the doctors back home. They refused to listen to my requests and insisted on calling me 'she' and 'her.' They stuck me in a dress, something I hadn't been forced to wear since I was a wee child. For some reason my body parts meant more to those doctors than what I'd always known—that I was a man."

And there goes Gareth Gunner. He walks away so fast he trips over himself.

Almost there, Amos. Deep breath. "Word got out I wasn't the man everyone thought I was, that I was being held against my will as a woman, and you know what? Men with whom I'd fought in the war came by and they set those doctors straight. Those men I'd fought with side by side, they *knew* who I was, and no doctor was going to tell them otherwise.

"When I passed on a few years later, I was buried in my full military uniform. My tombstone proudly says my name—'Albert D. J. Cashier'—the name I chose and loved.

I may not have come into this world looking the way some people might expect a man to, but I left it with people I cared for seeing me for who I really was."

I take off the cap and drop the accent. "It's me again—Amos." The crowd is eerily quiet. "I'm not trans, and there's no way to know for sure if that's how Albert would have identified but going off how he lived—there's a whole lot of evidence to say he would have called himself a trans man. As a young queer person, knowing Albert existed gives me hope. It connects me to the past in ways I've never known. Ways I didn't think were possible. It makes me feel seen. And Albert? He wasn't alone."

On cue, Jessica and Trish start strumming. A slow, bright tune.

I place the cap back on my head. In my Albert accent I say, "We are the LGBTQ+ voices of the past, and today, we will not be forgotten."

Ms. Wiseman steps forward. "I am Kitty Ely."

Right on her heels, Jessica says, "I am Charlotte Cushman."

Azul beams. "I am Alphons Richter."

Their names flood the stage.

"I am Carl Becker."

"I am Sarah Jewett."

"I am Mrs. Noonan."

"I am Emma Stebbins."

"I am Franklin Thompson."

"I am Harriet Hosmer."

"I am Amy Lowell."

"I am Joshua Speed."

"I am Addie Brown."

"I am Renée Vivien."

"I am Walt Whitman."

"I am Rose Cleveland."

"I am Matilda Hayes."

"I am Rebecca Primus."

"I am Herman Melville."

"I am Helen Emory."

"I am Mary Edmonia Lewis."

"I am David Derickson."

"I am James A. Garfield."

"I am Rosalie Sully."

Between the crescendo of names and music, I'm pretty much a giant goose bump by the time Ben is standing next to me in his suit, his fake brown beard hanging down his chin, his stovepipe hat just a little crooked. And he says, "I am Abraham Lincoln."

Someone actually gasps, and I almost start laughing. Not just because it's funny, but because I'm so freaking happy.

After Ben speaks, I grip the microphone again. Back to my regular voice, I say, "LGBTQ+ people especially, and everyone really, need to know about the amazing queer people who came before us. My friends and I, we've only begun the work, and so much of what we found was about white history. I know there are so many more stories about Black people, Indigenous people, and other people of color left for us to find. For too long we've listened to one narrative, one perspective of history. But today, we ask you to challenge the histories you've been told. Look for answers to the questions you didn't know you should be asking. Find the people who didn't make it into your textbooks. They deserve to be known. Thank you."

I duck back a step and we all join hands. Jessica and Trish pause their strumming to join hands with the others. I've got Ben on my left, Chloe on my right. We bow as one to the silent crowd.

Clap.

Clap. Clap. Clap.

I can breathe again.

Applause. From *multiple* people. For me. For us.

For Albert.

I thought I was happy before, but now I'm out of my mind. Jessica and Trish break into a fast, twangy song, and we all hoot, holler, and dance off the back of the stage. Soon as my feet reach the grass, Ms. Wiseman wraps me in an enormous hug. "Thank you," I say. "For everything."

The next second, Chloe is spinning me round. "You were freaking amazing!"

Azul, Cassidy, and Kevin are off laughing at each other. The other GSA kids are taking selfies in their costumes. Jessica and Trish give their guitars a final strum and are the last ones to head off the stage.

Ben's hand is on my shoulder. I think I'd like it to stay there forever. Yes, forever would be nice. He says, "I can't believe I just did that!"

I put my hand on his. "I can."

Ms. Wiseman dabs the corner of her eye. "I am so proud of you, Amos."

I'm shaking. I didn't realize how badly I was trembling until now. I take a seat in the grass.

"You okay?" Ben asks.

I inhale. "Took more out of me than I thought it would."

Ms. Wiseman tucks her handkerchief back into her dress. "Changing the world usually does."

35

Friday, August 12, 2022

Dear Albert,

Tomorrow's the big day. I'm kind of sort of freaking out. I texted the Gay Cerberus to make sure the GSA kids remember when to show up. Azul said they're good to go. I checked in with Jessica and Trish on Sunday. They're all set. And Chloe and Ms. Wiseman will be there with me all day, so that's one less thing to worry about.

So long as Mom doesn't find out, we should be good.

But I'm still nervous. And a little sad. And I did something I shouldn't have done.

I texted Ben.

I KNOW, ALBERT, I KNOW.

But he deserves to know. All of this is happening because of him just as much as it's happening because of me or Chloe or Ms. Wiseman. Here's what I said:

Hi, Ben. I know you probably hate me, but I thought you should know that tomorrow some friends, Chloe, and I are going to bring our proposal to life at the LHP. We're dressing up as our nineteenth-century queer American icons and taking a stand. It's sort of a secret. But I still thought you should know. And I wish you could be there.

I hit send after editing it seventy million times.

And now I'm sitting here, staring at my phone because I can't sleep and I keep thinking, maybe, maybe, MAYBE he'll text me back.

Since I'm waiting and already in a confessing kind of mood, I might as well mention that some annoying part of me must REALLY want Ben to show up tomorrow because I couldn't bring myself to cast someone as Abraham Lincoln for the performance. Obviously, Abraham Lincoln's potential queerness is SUPER important, but having him onstage without Ben being there—it just wouldn't be right, which totally sucks because I think people would have flipped out hearing Lincoln's name.

The closer I get to tomorrow, the more I wonder if *I'll* be ruining things for Mom for forever. If this performance goes south, she could lose her job . . . but this is what happens when you don't listen, right? People take action. Voices find a way to be heard, even if that means breaking a few rules.

Jobs aren't more important than human lives. No matter what happens tomorrow, Albert, I'm proud that I haven't stopped fighting. For you. For me. For Chloe.

For Ben.

It's been five hours.

He's not going to text me back, Albert, is he?

I don't know why I keep trying.

Good night,

Amos

36

★ ★ ★

Main Stage
Saturday, August 13, 2022—3:17 p.m.

I'm barely back to standing when Mom, Darren, Meredith, and Mr. Simmons round the corner. I brace for impact.

"What the hell was that liberal propaganda?" Mr. Simmons fumes. His eyes can't seem to decide where to glare—Ms. Wiseman, Mom, or me.

Ms. Wiseman steps in front of me, but Mom raises a hand. "I've got this, Ms. Wiseman."

"Mom." The word comes out somewhere between a plea and an apology. Every good thing I felt seconds ago is gone.

Her focus stays firmly on Mr. Simmons, but her hand rests on my shoulder. "This is not your park to run, Mr. Simmons. And my son isn't spouting 'liberal propaganda'—he shared well-researched, unadulterated truth. Had you read his proposal last fall you'd know that."

I do a double take. Mom's face is serious. And she's defending me. To *Mr. Simmons.*

"We have families sitting out there, and that"—he jabs his finger at me—"*that* was not family-friendly content. I expect better from you, Hannah."

There he goes, attacking Mom for standing with me. I hate that she was right to be worried. I hate that he made me lie to my mom. And I can't take it anymore. I yell, "Mom didn't know. None of this is her fault."

Mom steps closer to me. She says softly, "Amos, honey, I knew."

"What?" I back up a step.

Mr. Simmons fumes. "Excuse me?"

Ms. Wiseman looks apologetically at me. "It wouldn't have been right for me not to tell her. And your mom—"

"Your mom is proud of what you accomplished up there," Mom says. "Honestly, I'm ashamed I didn't think about offering you the spot myself."

I flush. "I—if you knew, why didn't you say anything?"

The wrinkles deepen around her eyes. "I was hoping you'd tell me on your own, but the closer we got to today, the more I realized just how much I'd shaken your faith in me. I'm sorry, Amos. There's no battle I won't fight for you."

My eyes sting. "I'm sorry I didn't tell you, Mom."

"You don't need to apologize." She hugs me. "We're in this together."

Mr. Simmons coughs. "Look, you can have your little rainbow lovefest, but the board is going to hear about this.

Our organization stands for traditional American values, and we don't need your leftist, revisionist, brainwashed kid—"

"That's enough, Derek." Mom's voice cuts his whining short. "You will not attack my son's character, and you do not decide what's best for this organization. *I* am in charge, not you."

"We'll see how much longer that lasts."

Oh, crap. This is what I was afraid of. She can't lose her job because of me. "Mr. Simmons," I cut in, "I'm sorry if what we presented wasn't what you were expecting, but it meant a lot to me, and all of it was true. I'm not trying to change history—I'm trying to share more of it. Albert deserves that, and so do kids like me. Everyone should feel like they belong at the LHP."

Mr. Simmons pulls himself together. "Everyone *is* welcome at the Living History Park, Amos. That doesn't mean you get to rewrite the past to make yourself feel better. Your accusations of transgenderism and homosexuality—"

"No disrespect, Mr. Simmons, but sometimes history needs to be rewritten." Chloe grabs hold of my hand. "So many stories are missing. Black stories, queer stories, *queer Black* stories! What about Native Americans? What about identities we haven't even thought to think of yet? It's about time we added them in."

Ms. Wiseman adds, "She's right. Important details can

270

be left out. Prejudices and biases get in the way of honesty. You know, it's not so much history being rewritten as it is history being *righted.*"

"Who said you get to decide what's right?" says Mr. Simmons.

Chloe glares. "Do I have to remind you about the photo in the gallery, Mr. Simmons?"

Red spills into his cheeks. "Chloe, the board has already taken corrective measures to adjust the plaque beneath the photo with the, um, boy and soldier."

"You can call him Black," she says. "A young, enslaved Black boy and a free, white Union soldier."

"Right." Mr. Simmons fiddles with a button on his sweat-damp polo. "But these are not what we're talking about right now."

"You're right," I say. "Race and gender and sexuality aren't the same things. But seeing yourself accurately represented in history and the world you live in—that's what connects people from all sorts of backgrounds and identities together. Making sure everyone who comes to the LHP feels seen is more important than worrying about offending someone."

"Or shoes," Ben mutters.

I could kiss him.

Like, for real this time.

"Uh, excuse me?" A Black man with dark brown skin

and a thin mustache pokes his head around the edge of the stage. Beneath him is a young Black boy with short, dark hair. We all turn to look at the newcomers.

"Sorry if we're interrupting," the man says, "but my son was wondering if we could talk to him"—he points at me—"for a minute?"

"Now's not the best time," Mr. Simmons says, "but if you need to file a complaint, there's a link on our websi—"

The father waves his hand at Mr. Simmons with a chuckle. "No, no. It's nothing like that."

Curious, and *so* over Mr. Simmons and his bigotry, I approach the man and his son. He can't be more than eight or nine and is adorable. His skin, a little darker than his father's, is smooth and unblemished. He's wearing a Pokémon tank top and khaki shorts. A rainbow friendship bracelet dangles from his wrist. I kneel down so we're eye to eye.

"What's your name?"

"Caleb," he says, twisting on his heels like he's embarrassed.

"What did you want to talk about?"

Caleb glances nervously up at his father. He pats his son's back and says, "You can tell him. It's all right."

Reassured, Caleb smiles and leans closer. "I'm trans, like Albert."

"He came out to us last year," his father explains. "We've been on this journey together, haven't we, Caleb?"

He nods. "I liked hearing about Albert. I didn't know people like me could have fought in the Civil War."

"I'm so glad." My heart is bursting. Like, actually exploding in my chest. "People like you have been doing amazing things for a long, long time. Albert is pretty incredible, isn't he?"

"Yeah."

His father places his hands on his son's shoulders. "We just—" A tear is budding on his eyelid. "We just wanted to say thank you. Your speech was, um, a pleasant surprise." He pauses, wiping the tear away. "No. More than that. It was a blessing."

His hand stretches toward me. We shake. His grip is strong but kind, too. Then Caleb and his father say goodbye. Our small group is alone again. I'm overwhelmed. There are no words for what just happened.

Someone grabs my bicep. Ben. "Amos, *you* did that. You gave that little boy hope. You made him feel seen."

My chest swells. "It wasn't me. It was Albert."

Mom, Ms. Wiseman, Ben, and Chloe are all smiles.

Behind them, Mr. Simmons clears his throat. "That doesn't change anything."

"Maybe not," Mom says, "but it's a start. I am so proud of you, Amos. And you, Chloe." Her eyes linger on Ben. "Even you, Mr. Oglevie. Happy to see you, I think." She grabs my hand. "You kids really are the future."

Ben blushes. I throw my right arm around his shoulders and pull Chloe close with my left.

"A bright future, indeed," Ms. Wiseman agrees.

Mom thumbs dirt from my cheek. "How about we celebrate? Elephant ears on me."

We leave Meredith and Mr. Simmons backstage, alone and silent.

I don't look back.

37

Sunday, September 18, 2022

Dear Albert,

Life has been BANANAS. So much has been going on (starting my first year of HIGH SCHOOL) that I haven't had much time to write. Sorry about that. Time for an Amos Abernathy update of epic proportions. Hope you're ready!

Okay, so, last time I wrote to you was . . . oh my God. The night before our performance at Civil War Remembrance Week! AH! Wow, I've really been a terrible pen pal.

Let's start with Mom. She tried not to let it show, but I could tell she was worried about losing her job. Mr. Simmons and a few of the other board members who heard about what happened made a stink, but when the board finally met to discuss "the incident," aka Our Incredible Performance, the outcome wasn't quite what Mom, Mr. Simmons, or any of us expected.

Apparently, the board received several emails about what we did, and not all of them were supportive, but the kind, encouraging, appreciative emails far outweighed the negative ones, or so I hear. Caleb and his father were among them, praising the Living History Park for its "inclusive efforts" and "paving the way to make a difference in the lives of LGBTQ+ youth."

Pastor Shirt wrote an opinion piece that ended up in the *Chickaree County Herald*. His article was titled "History Transformed and Transformative: What Our Youth Can Teach Us About the Past." Here's a bit of what he had to say.

I've known Amos Abernathy most of his life. I've watched him grow up and come into his own, becoming the tremendous young man who is working hard to change the way we think about the people who have come before us.

Hard as it is to admit, I've never given history much thought in terms of marginalized communities. As a white man married to a woman, I've seen myself accurately reflected in history books all my life. Granted, much of my ancestors' history is rife with problems, but it's there. I know men like me existed and that, for millennia, we've been messing up and trying to do better.

What Amos illuminated for me is that I'm only seeing a segment of history, a fragmented narrative largely told by privileged white men that carelessly, and often

intentionally, leaves out the stories of people with iden-
tities that differ from their own.

Amos also helped me realize that I don't ask enough
questions. Most all my life, I have blindly accepted what
was written in history books and taught in classes. I
didn't think to ask if there was more to the story.

I am now, Amos. I'm researching. I'm reconsider-
ing. I'm leaving space for possibility. For this, I thank
you.

Pastor Shirt didn't stop there. He wrote the board a letter commending them on their forward-thinking efforts and praising me and Mom for our bravery.

Needless to say, Mom didn't get canned. Mr. Simmons and Meredith are still bitter, but you can't win every battle, right?

Like I said earlier, the new school year started a few weeks ago. Freshman year. I seriously can't believe I'm in HIGH SCHOOL. The building is so much bigger, and I almost have to run to make it to seventh period on time, but I like it for the most part.

I keep in touch with Ms. Wiseman. Mom and her have actually become pretty good friends. She invited Ms. Wiseman and Nadia over for dinner last week. Considering that Darren has been eating dinner with us for a while, it wasn't too weird adding another teacher to the mix.

On the other hand, I see Chloe way less than I did last year. She's taking a bunch of accelerated classes and even an AP class. Not really my speed, but she's loving it.

I might not see Chloe as much, but guess who I *do* see in class?

Ben.

Freaking Ben Oglevie.

It took until the very last second, but he finally convinced his parents to let him go to public high school.

On our first day, his first words were, "There's so many people."

"Oh, more than at home?" I smirked.

"Just a few."

His parents were worried he'd have trouble adjusting. Let me tell you, Albert, Ben hasn't had *any* problems. He tried out for track, joined the after-school jazz choir, and aced his first biology test.

If anyone is having trouble adjusting, it's me. Now Ben's in my space all the time, and it's great, but we're still figuring out how to be us. He knows I have feelings for him, but his parents don't want him to date yet, and, honestly, I don't think Mom is too keen on me dating anyone either. I keep telling her I'm in HIGH SCHOOL. High schoolers date. All the time. Why not me?

But learning to be friends—*just* friends—with someone you want to be more than friends with is like being forced to eat steamed spinach even though the cheesiest pizza in the world is sitting in front of you.

Ben and I haven't talked about *feelings* since this summer. He hasn't brought anything up, and I don't know what else there is to say. I hate to think that, after all of this, we're destined to just be friends. I mean, I do still want to be his friend, if that's what he wants. I GUESS I'LL JUST HAVE TO DEAL WITH HIM BEING THE CHEESIEST PIZZA IN THE WORLD.

Anyway . . . aside from high school and Ben, I'm figuring out what comes next for me. If I've learned anything over the past year, it's that I like having a project. Maybe I'll start researching queer people in other eras. Maybe I'll make a website with all the information I find. The Gender and Sexuality Alliance at our high school is even bigger. I bet I could recruit some more help.

All in all, Albert, things are looking up for Amos Abernathy, and I have you to thank. I know it sounds ridiculous, and that wherever you are—heaven or who knows—you might not get this, but, Albert, you got me through this year. Thank you for living your truth when the world was in such a dark place. Thank you for serving our country. Thank you for existing.

You've given me hope. You've given me possibility. I know I can never repay you for that. I hope honoring your memory is a start.

And, if you don't mind, I think I might keep writing to you every once in a while.

Just to say hi.

Or who knows—there might be more wars that need fighting.

Your friend,

Amos Abernathy

38

Friday, September 30, 2022

Dear Albert,

Ben asked me to Homecoming.

Freaking Ben Oglevie asked ME to Homecoming.

Okay.

That is all.

Your friend,

Amos Abernathy

AUTHOR'S NOTE

Write what you know. That's what my mom told me growing up, but I was too busy telling stories about magic and fantastical creatures. It wasn't until after graduate school that something shifted inside me and her words made sense. Finally, at nearly thirty years old, I was ready to write something personal. Something close to my heart.

Like Amos, I know what it's like to be openly gay and proud of my identity. Like Ben, I know what it is like to be afraid to come out as a young person. From about fourth to seventh grade, I volunteered as a nineteenth-century historical reenactor. Ben and I also share a history of being homeschooled, though my educational experience was far more complicated than his. I wanted to bring these experiences that shaped me together in a story, but I didn't know how to do that until I realized something else: as much as I needed to write what I know, I also needed to write what I *didn't* know.

The more I thought about it, the more apparent it became that I didn't know quite a lot. Why didn't I know more about LGBTQ+ people from before the early 1900s? Why hadn't I read anything about queer historical figures in my textbooks? Where was the history of people like me? In that moment I realized that Amos, Ben, and I all had the same questions: Could we have existed back then? Did any LGBTQ+ people fight in the Civil War? If they did, why didn't I know about them?

Like most people with a question, I went straight to Google. My search results were almost identical to what Amos experiences. Initially there was more information about queer European history than American. I adjusted my keywords. History about queer Americans began to trickle through, but I wasn't satisfied. I wanted to know if there was someone close to home, someone from Illinois. It wasn't until I searched "queer Civil War soldier Illinois" that everything changed. Albert D. J. Cashier's Wikipedia page was the first result. I read the entry and leaped down the rabbit hole, looking for anything and everything about this man.

I scoured the web for additional primary and secondary sources, not just about Albert but about the Civil War, the enslavement of Black people, American life during the nineteenth century, and other queer people who lived at that time. I quickly came to understand that sexual orientation

284

and gender identity were thought of in very different terms in nineteenth-century America than they are today. Defining gender and sexual identity wasn't going to be simple or straightforward. I would have to interpret facts to the best of my ability. For example, I concluded that Abraham Lincoln was part of the LGBTQ+ community because of the evidence I was able to find, not because his sexual identity was explicitly stated.

The more I learned about Albert, Lincoln, and the complicated history of gender and sexual identity, the more I realized that this story was going to be bigger than showing and celebrating the existence of gay boys and men; it had to be about the LGBTQ+ community at large.

I continued my research. I read books from my local library and consulted with expert librarians at Vermont College of Fine Arts. I took my research on the road and visited the Naper Settlement, which is a historical center in Naperville, Illinois, that partially inspired the Living History Park in this novel, and Albert D. J. Cashier's home and gravesite in Saunemin, Illinois.

The historical information in this novel, including everything Amos learns and shares about Albert's life, is as accurate as possible. Albert was assigned female at birth and was an Irish immigrant who lived in Belvidere and then Saunemin, Illinois. He served for three years in the Union army during the American Civil War, used he/him pronouns, and lived his life as a man. He was beloved by his community then and is still fondly remembered today, his memory passed down generation to generation.

In all of my researching, I consulted numerous sources. Sometimes information varied depending on who was telling the story. When I found differing facts, I went with what I believe is the more reliable source or what the majority of sources agree upon.

If you want to learn more about Albert D. J. Cashier, the American Civil War, nineteenth-century America, LGBTQ+ and BIPOC American history, and other historical figures mentioned in this novel, I've listed some resources here for further exploration.

I hope you leave this novel asking your own questions. One book can never provide you with all the answers. What questions did Amos and I *not* ask? What questions still need to be answered? What would you need to do to find those answers? Whose story needs to be told? Whose voice does the world need to hear?

"ALBERT D. J. CASHIER'S HOME IN SAUNEMIN, IL" PHOTO CREDIT: MICHAEL LEALI

"ALBERT D. J. CASHIER'S HEADSTONE IN SAUNEMIN, IL" PHOTO CREDIT: MICHAEL LEALI

★ ABOUT ALBERT D. J. CASHIER ★

American Battlefield Trust: www.battlefields.org/learn/biographie /albert-cashier

Saunemin, Illinois's Albert D. J. Cashier Website: www.sites.google.com /site/albertdjcashier/home

Sanders, Rob, and Nabi Ali. *The Fighting Infantryman: The Story of Albert D. J. Cashier, Transgender Civil War Soldier.* New York: Little Bee Books, 2020.

★ ABOUT NINETEENTH-CENTURY LGBTQ+ AMERICANS ★

The Library Company of Philadelphia: www.librarycompany.org/gayatlcp

Connecticut History: www.connecticuthistory.org/the-lives-of-addie -brown-and-rebecca-primus-told-through-their-loving-letters

Library of Congress: "A Complicated Case": https://chroniclingamerica. loc.gov/lccn/sn85042331/1878-11-04/ed-1/seq-1/

Outhistory.org: www.outhistory.org/exhibits/show/aspectsofqueerexis- tence/intro

★ ABOUT BIPOC NINETEENTH-CENTURY AMERICANS ★

American Battlefield Trust:

www.battlefields.org/learn/videos/black-soldiers-civil-war
www.battlefields.org/learn/articles/black-confederates-truth-and-legend

Illinois.gov: www2.illinois.gov/dnrhistoric/Research/pages/afamhist.aspx

Horwitz, Tony. *Confederates in the Attic: Dispatches from the Unfinished Civil War*. New York: Vintage Books, 1999.

Lincoln, Abraham. *Abraham Lincoln: Complete Works*. Edited by John G. Nicolay and John Hay. Arkose Press, 2015.

Sullivan, George, and Mathew B. Brady. *In the Wake of Battle: The Civil War Images of Mathew Brady*. Munich: Prestel Publishing Ltd., 2004.

ACKNOWLEDGMENTS

Dear Reader,

My name might be on the cover, but this book wouldn't be here without the incredible work of so many talented, wise, and gracious people to whom I am forever grateful.

To Sara Crowe, my wonderful agent, who adored Amos right from the get-go, thank you. I am so appreciative of all the Pippins—Holly McGhee, Elena Giovinazzo, Cameron Chase, and Rakeem Nelson.

Words cannot fully express how much I cherish my brilliant editor, Stephanie Stein, who believed in me and this story, and helped make it the best possible version of itself. You are a gift.

My gratitude extends to so many others at Harper-Collins as well, especially Louisa Currigan, Jon Howard, Gwen Morton, Martha Schwartz, Sean Cavanagh, Vanessa Nuttry, Corina Lupp, Alison Klapthor, Delaney Heisterkamp, Patty Rosati, Mimi Rankin, Katie Dutton, and the tremendously talented Ariel Vittori for this beautiful cover.

My deepest thanks to Alaysia Jordan for her insightful
and invaluable feedback that helped me see where the story
should grow and change.

A very special thank you to Al Arnolts, who shared his
passion for Albert D. J. Cashier with me, offering a tour of
Albert's home and gravesite.

I am so grateful to the friends I have made in the library,
bookselling, and publishing worlds. You all are rock stars.
Kathleen March, I simply adore you and the gifts of enthusiasm and joy you bring to sharing books with readers. Lizzie
Lewandowski, Jackie Douglas, and Mallory Hyde, thank
you for your constant love and support. Valerie Pierce,
Margaret Coffee, and Tiffany Schultz, your friendship and
belief in me means the world.

I am eternally grateful to the Vermont College of Fine
Arts community, especially my fellow Guardians of Literary
Mischief. Without you, I simply wouldn't be here today. To
all the faculty at VCFA, especially Will Alexander, David
Gill, Kekla Magoon, and Amy King—thank you for showing
me that I do belong here. Thank you to the VCFA library
wizards, especially Lennie DeCerce and Bianca Vinas, who
aided me in my early research. My unending love and appre-
ciation to my critique partners and friends, Adina Baseler
and Sarah Willis—I cannot wait for readers to get their
hands on your stories. Thank you, Max Bronson, for being

my continual support and dear friend. The Beverly Shores crew, thank you for inviting me in and loving me through so much. To my Saturday morning writing group—Sarah Aronson, Tegan Beese, Alina Borger-Germann, Deborah King, Jen Loescher, JP McCormick, Erin Nuttall, Denise Santomauro, Skyler Schrempp, Libby Wheeler, and Mary Winn Heider: I love you all so very much, and that is the turth.

Many teachers made a tremendous impact on my early writing life, but two stand out. First, Krista Neitzel, who in eighth grade let me write a fantasy story in three parts while other kids wrote . . . something else. And then, over summer break, she read a full fantasy manuscript of mine, commenting in the margins throughout! You helped me believe I could really tell stories. And to my mom, who was my first teacher, my first reader, my first champion. Thank you for instilling a love of writing and storytelling in me from such an early age.

There have been so many friends who have stood by me as I've been on this writing journey. I am beyond grateful to all my cheerleaders. Many hugs to my colleagues and friends Karen Ferguson, Erin Holtz, Amy Howerton, Chanel Keyvan, Kristin Lavelle, Emily Popp, Erica Russell, and Frank Tieri. And all my love to my dear friends Cori Veverka, Renee Niederkorn, Sean and Christy Tait, and

Brian and Genna Brems.

Thank you to my students who inspire me and teach me more than they will ever realize.

I want to extend tremendous gratitude to all of my family. Thank you to my grandparents Nick and Andrea Polizzi, who made pursuing this dream a reality; you were the best grad school roommates a guy could ask for. To my siblings, Niko, Zachary, and Annabelle, and their partners, Becky, Lexi, and Corbin—thank you for loving me, for laughter, and for standing by my side. And to my parents, Mike and Danine, who have loved me, supported me, guided me, and helped shape me into the person I am today—thank you. I love you all to the moon and back.

Dear Albert D. J. Cashier, I am so grateful that I got to learn about you and share your story. You will forever be in my heart.

And lastly, dear reader, thank you. I am so, so grateful for your time, attention, and caring. Keep reading, keep learning, keep loving.

Your friend,

Michael Leali